Ready . . . set . . . go!

Croakbag the Raven is off to the races!

Kraaaark!

Jeremy Strong once worked in a bakery, putting the jam into three thousand doughnuts every night. Now he puts the jam in stories instead, which he finds much more exciting. At the age of three, he fell out of a first-floor bedroom window and landed on his head. His mother says that this damaged him for the rest of his life and refuses to take any responsibility. He loves writing stories because he says it is 'the only time you alone have complete control and can make anything happen'. His ambition is to make you laugh (or at least snuffle). Jeremy Strong lives near Bath with his wife, Gillie, two cats, two hens and a flying cow.

www.jeremystrong.co.uk

ARE YOU FEELING SILLY ENOUGH TO READ MORE?

**THE BEAK SPEAKS
BEWARE! KILLER TOMATOES
CHICKEN SCHOOL
DINOSAUR POX
GIANT JIM AND THE HURRICANE
KRAZY KOW SAVES THE WORLD – WELL, ALMOST
THERE'S A PHARAOH IN OUR BATH!**

**JEREMY STRONG'S LAUGH-YOUR-SOCKS-OFF JOKE BOOK
JEREMY STRONG'S LAUGH-YOUR-SOCKS-OFF EVEN MORE JOKE BOOK**

**The Hundred-Mile-An-Hour Dog series
THE HUNDRED-MILE-AN-HOUR DOG
CHRISTMAS CHAOS FOR THE HUNDRED-MILE-AN-HOUR DOG
LOST! THE HUNDRED-MILE-AN-HOUR DOG
THE HUNDRED-MILE-AN-HOUR DOG GOES FOR GOLD**

**My Brother's Famous Bottom series
MY BROTHER'S FAMOUS BOTTOM
MY BROTHER'S HOT CROSS BOTTOM
MY BROTHER'S FAMOUS BOTTOM GETS PINCHED
MY BROTHER'S FAMOUS BOTTOM GOES CAMPING**

THE KING OF COMEDY

Jeremy STRONG

ROMANS on the RAMPAGE!

CHARIOT CHAMPIONS!

Illustrated by Rowan Clifford

PUFFIN

PUFFIN BOOKS

UK | USA | Canada | Ireland | Australia
India | New Zealand | South Africa

Puffin Books is part of the Penguin Random House group of companies
whose addresses can be found at global.penguinrandomhouse.com.

www.penguin.co.uk
www.puffin.co.uk
www.ladybird.co.uk

First published 2017
001

Text copyright © Jeremy Strong, 2017
Illustrations copyright © Rowan Clifford, 2017

The moral right of the author and illustrator has been asserted

Set in Baskerville MT
Printed in Great Britain by Clays Ltd, St Ives plc

A CIP catalogue record for this book is available from the British Library

ISBN: 978–0–141–37255–6

*This story is dedicated to one of
my most favourite cities – Rome.*

Contents

Introduction   1

1. Lots of Questions and Not Many Answers   5

2. Elephant Stuff   16

3. Phew! Things Never Stop Happening,
   Do They?   29

4. One in a Million?   42

5. The Lunatic Professor Gets Lucky!   54

6. The Goat is Redundant   67

7. A Wedding   79

8. What's the Smelliest Stuff in the World?   91

9. Dust! Wind! Hooves! Noise!   103

10. GOGOGOGOGOGOGOGO!!!   116

11. Be Patient!   129

12. Marriage? What Marriage?
    Whose Marriage?   140

12½. All Done and Dusted.
    Go on, Give Us a Biscuit!   153

Introduction

Hello! It's me, Croakbag – the cleverest raven in the Roman Empire. **Krraaarrkk!** Give us a biscuit! Whaddya mean, am I a talking bird? Can fish swim? Do frogs jump? Of course I can talk, and have I got a story for you. Oh yes! I am *Corvus maximus intelligentissimus*. That's your actual Latin, that is, and it means 'a very brainy raven' – in other words, ME!

So, *salve*, ladies, gentlemen and pipsqueaks. Do you know what *salve* means? Yes, you do. That's right! It means 'hello' in the old Latin. Just try that out on your mum and I bet she'll swoon with admiration and think you are the smartest youngster on the planet. On the other hand, she might simply stand there looking completely baffled, in which case you can explain, 'I am speaking Latin, *Mater*,' because *mater* means 'mother'. Aren't you a clever clogs? Yes, you are. Have a biscuit.

BUT, I can't waste any more time on greetings and what-not. It's down to business and there's lots to explain. You're in for a real helter-skelter of a story.

Our hero, Perilus, 11, dreams of being a charioteer like his friend and hero, Scorcha. But Perilus is facing a BIG problem – and he doesn't even know it yet. His mum and dad (Krysis and Flavia) are stuck in jail, along with the two family slaves, Flippus Floppus and Fussia, and a good and kindly neighbour, Trendia. None of them have done anything wrong. It's just one GINORMOUS MISTAKE, made even worse by the fact that the

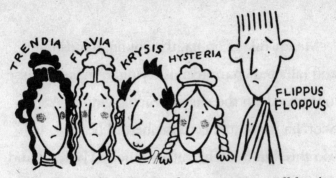

TRENDIA FLAVIA KRYSIS HYSTERIA FLIPPUS FLOPPUS

prison guards have got only one very small brain between them and they seem to have managed to lose even that.

Krysis has been accused of stealing 10,000 silver denarii from the Emperor's bank. Did he do it? Of course not, but now Krysis has to find out who DID do it and prove that he, Krysis, is innocent. Which he is, because he's a decent sort of chap on the whole, when he's not shouting at Perilus or trying to marry his daughter, Hysteria, off to some ancient heap of wrinkles with brown teeth and no hair. **Kraaarrk!** It's a tough life being a teenage girl in ancient Rome, I can tell you. No wonder Hysteria spends half her time in tears. Her little bro, Perilus, calls her The Waterfall On Legs.

Meanwhile Scorcha, the young, handsome and talented charioteer, is trying to make a name for himself on the chariot-racing circuit. And Scorcha is not just Perilus's hero. I blush to tell you this, but Scorcha rather fancies Hysteria and she just happens to fancy him back. (Ah! Isn't that cute?) But she hasn't dared tell him. (OK, I'm going to be sick now.) However, her father, Krysis, is trying to sell Hysteria off as a bride to Fibbus Biggus, who isn't very nice. (Remember the brown teeth?) Poor Hysteria; no wonder she's in tears. But Krysis knows that if Hysteria's not married off by the time she's fourteen or fifteen, people in Rome will not be impressed. Bad parenting, that's what they'll say.

Anyway, we must get on! Plunge in! And hold tight to your cozzie!

1. Lots of Questions and
   Not Many Answers

There was only one living creature in the whole
of Rome who could sort this mess out and it just
so happened that the one living creature was me.
I am Croakbag, *Corvus supremus, Corvus brainia
giganticus, Corvus smartia-pantius.*

I settled on a roof top with a nice bit of dead
squirrel to chew while I made a to-do list in my
head. It went something like this:

  1. Find Perilus and Hysteria and tell
  them their mum and dad are in jail.
  2. Get Krysis, Flavia and everyone else
  out of jail, but how?
  3. Find the robber who stole the 10,000
  silver denarii.

4. Tell the Emperor, Tyrannus.

5. Save Hysteria from being married off
to Fibbus Biggus, but how?

6. Find some more dead squirrel. (This
had nothing to do with 1, 2, 3, 4 or 5, but
I was still feeling hungry.)

As you can see, it was quite a long list and
there was a bit of a hurry on so I went flapping
off to find Perilus, which actually meant finding
an elephant. Perilus has made friends with a stray
elephant. She just sort of turned up one day and
began following Perilus around. Her name is
Tiddles. I'll let you guess why.

I was flapping about. Wings are very useful,
you know, especially for flying. You can get
right up high and look down on everything and
everyone and I like looking down on everyone.
Hurr hurr hurr!

There was the whole of Rome spread out
below and it didn't take me long to spy out an

elephant splashing about in the Tiber. (That's
the river that flows through Rome. See? You're
picking up geography now, as well as Latin.)

I went swooping down and landed on Tiddles's
head. Perilus was sitting on the river bank,
throwing stones at a drifting log.

'*Salve*, Perilus! I have news for you. Your mum
and dad are in jail.'

Perilus leaped to his feet, ready for action.
That's my boy!

'Where? How? Why? Who? When? How? Who?'

'Slow down! You've asked half of those once already. Don't get your toga in a twist. Take it easy. You know what those guards are like at the jail.'

'Stupid!' Perilus shouted, stamping his feet.

'Yes, exactly. Flippus Floppus and Trendia are in jail with them.'

'Ridiculous!' cried Perilus. 'We must get them out! I'll fight the guards.'

I am very fond of Perilus but he is a bit of a hothead. He goes charging in and putting himself in danger without really thinking. No, if you need a thinker, you don't want Perilus. You want someone like − *er-hrrrm* (that's me clearing my throat) − someone like ME! And I just happened to be there, so that was very convenient, wasn't it?

Whaddya mean, I'm a show-off? I am simply giving you the facts. I happen to be immensely brainy. That's not my fault. It's how I was born − *biggus brainius.*

So I pointed one feathery wing tip at Tiddles. 'That,' I declared, 'is our key to the jail.'

'No, it isn't,' Perilus quibbled. 'It's an elephant.'

'I know that, young master, but elephants are big and strong. Imagine what might happen if Tiddles just happened to lean against that jail door.'

Perilus's eyes lit up. 'Brilliant! But we still have to get past the guards.'

'I think your sister can manage that for us. Where is she?'

'I haven't seen her since she went off to watch Scorcha at the races.'

'She's probably still there. You head to the jail and we will meet you there. *Vale!*'

'*Vale!*' cried Perilus, and now you know the Latin for 'goodbye' as well as 'hello'. Aren't you learning fast?

It was quite easy to find Hysteria. She was still at the circus. (Now listen, it is not *that* kind of circus. The circus is where chariot races are held in Rome.) Anyhow, there was Hysteria and there was Scorcha and they were simply staring at each other and HOLDING HANDS! You could almost see two hearts fluttering as one. All very sweet. Unfortunately, it was certainly not something Krysis would have been pleased to see. Scorcha in love with his daughter? No, no, no, that wouldn't do. After all, Scorcha was an ex-slave. Highly-born young ladies don't marry ex-slaves. I could see yet another problem lying ahead.

I fluttered down and coughed quietly. Twice. They took no notice at all. So I croaked.

KRRAARRRKKKK!

That woke them up. Hysteria looked at me, her eyes shining like two little diamonds in a pool of pink jelly.

'Scorcha won his race!' she gushed. I shook my head hard. I hate gushing.

'Good. Listen, your father's in jail.'

'He's so clever, Croakbag!'

'I'm sure he is. Listen, Hysteria, your father is in jail and so is your mother.'

'Scorcha is so brave. I think he must be the bravest man in Rome.'

'I'm sure he is, but your parents are IN JAIL, you see, and so are Fussia and Flippus Floppus and Trendia.'

'I don't think I've ever met anyone as brave and clever as Scorcha,' said Hysteria, with a glushy-blushy sigh.

'EVERYONE'S IN JAIL AND ABOUT TO

HAVE THEIR HEADS CHOPPED OFF!' I
yelled.

Phew. At last. Hysteria began to look just
slightly alarmed. 'Mater and Pater are going to
be executed?' she asked.

'Well, probably not executed, Hysteria, but
they are in jail and we need to get them out.
Perilus is waitin' at the jail with Tiddles, but we
need your help too.'

'Should I come? I could help,' suggested
Scorcha.

'*Kraaarrk!* You stay here,' I told him. 'It's
not that long since we got you out of jail after
Crabbus had you arrested for almost destroyin'
his house, even though it wasn't exactly your
fault. Besides, you'll be too much of a distraction
for Hysteria. Come on, we must go, NOW.'

Hysteria glanced back at Scorcha, blew him
a kiss, blushed a very deep red and finally came
trotting after me.

'He's wonderful,' she told me as we hurried

towards the city jail. 'He can read and write.'

'Good,' I muttered. I must say that really was an achievement, considering about three-quarters of Rome couldn't read or write, especially the slave population. 'However, now we need to concentrate on gettin' your parents out of jail.'

'I love him, Croakbag.'

Ahh! Isn't that sweet? No, it's not! Get over it!

Hysteria looked so happy. In fact, I had never seen her looking so cheerful. Usually, being with Hysteria was like sitting next to a large squelchy marsh in the middle of the monsoon season, *ergo* wet.

Do you know that one? Yes, it's Latin and it means 'therefore', as demonstrated in this sentence: I, Croakbag the raven, am super-clever, *ergo* I will sort all this out.

We reached the jail and there was Perilus, along with Tiddles. The plan (my super-clever plan, of course) was for Hysteria to go ahead of us and distract the guards while we crept in unseen.

Please note those last three words – 'crept in unseen'. Have you ever tried creeping anywhere unseen WITH AN ELEPHANT? Probably you haven't. But I am quite sure that you will understand that trying to squeeze past four guards with a not-exactly-invisible pachyderm (that's such a great word for an elephant, isn't it? Stun your teacher with that one!) was going to be a tall order.

Anyhow, Hysteria put on her best smile and sauntered up to the guards while Perilus and Tiddles and I waited out of sight just around the corner. Hysteria began talking to the guards but they didn't budge. They were standing right across the entrance to the prison. I peered round the corner and watched. Perilus peered round the corner. Tiddles peered round the corner. Then the elephant stepped out into broad daylight. There she was – an entire elephant in full view of the guards.

2. Elephant Stuff

'Tiddles!' I hissed. 'Come back!' I did some
frantic beckoning with one wing but the
elephant simply ignored me. I cursed myself.
I knew it was never a good idea to work with
animals. They always mess up.

Tiddles seemed intent on getting a drink
of water from the nearby horse trough. She
wandered across, dipped in her trunk and took
a long, cool sip. Perilus and I watched in horror.
This was not going to plan at all.

That was when Hysteria did something
extraordinary. 'Oh look,' she said to the guards.
'There's an elephant behind you, filling her
trunk with water. I wonder why she's doing
that?'

One of the guards folded his arms across his

chest and snorted. 'Don't be daft. We're not going to fall for that old trick.'

'It's not a trick,' declared Hysteria. 'It's true, there's an elephant behind you.'

'Yeah yeah yeah, and then we all turn round and, while we're looking at the-elephant-that-isn't-there, you open the prison gates and let all the prisoners out.'

'Yeah,' chuckled the leader of the guards. 'She's completely ludicrous.'

'No, no, I'm Ludicrus,' declared the first guard. 'Ludicrus is my name.'

A third guard shook his head sadly. 'No, it's not plausible.'

'Hey!' cried their leader. 'I'm Plausible. Stop being ridiculous.'

'But I AM Ridiculus!' yelled the third guard.

'Right! Stop it!' bellowed the leader of the guards. 'For once, let's get this straight. I'm Plausible, you're Ridiculus and you're Ludicrus.'

All three nodded hard and then slowly, one by

one, all three heads turned to look at the fourth guard.

'So who are you?' they chorused.

'Namelus,' murmured the fourth guard.

Plausible clapped his hands. 'Brilliant! Sorted! Now then, what's the elephant called?'

'What elephant?' asked Ludicrus.

'The one behind us,' said Plausible. 'Hang on – an elephant? It IS an elephant! That's what the girl told us. A REAL ELEPHANT! HELLLLLPPP!'

Hurr hurr hurr! Aren't we having fun? Yes, we are. It was too late, anyhow. By this time Tiddles was fully tanked up with water and she let loose at the guards. Unfortunately, Hysteria got in the way a bit, but then she's used to being wet all over. However, the guards were blown off their feet, and as soon as they managed to scramble back the entirely unexpected sight of the elephant was enough to send them rushing home to their maters.

Perilus took the opportunity to climb on board Tiddles and guide her to the prison entrance, where our lovely pachyderm made short work of the gates and was soon treading them into the dust.

We hurried inside and quickly found Krysis and Flavia, Flippus and Fussia and, of course, Trendia. We set them free, along with most of the other prisoners. What a happy lot they were, and grateful too.

'If there's anything we can do for you, just let us know,' they said, which was very kind of them.

One of the prisoners was a short, stumpy kind of chap with a long nose and ears that stuck out. I was just thinking the poor man looked a bit like Tiddles when he sidled up to me.

'You with them?' he muttered, turning his nose towards Krysis and his family.

'I am,' I croaked.

'Anything I can do to help, just ask. Hear all sorts of stuff in prison.'

'Do you?'

The man nodded. 'I know him,' he added, looking at Krysis again. 'Used to be head of the Imperial Mint, didn't he? Oh yes, I know him. Don't forget. If you want help, you know where to come. The name's Blabbus. Got that? Hear all sorts of stuff in prison,' he repeated, tapping his nose with one finger. 'Oh yes.'

Then he slid away and vanished into the crowd of escaping prisoners. Well, that was interesting of course, but there were important things to get sorted and the most important one was to get my family safely away from the prison and the guards.

We marched home in triumph. Well, they

marched while I, being a raven, hopped, flapped and waddled home with them. Tiddles was the hero of the day, which was very nice for her. But really, I ask you, whose idea was it? MINE. Where was the gratitude? Nowhere. Gratitude was totally invisible, absent, missing and silent. Huh. Tiddles even got cuddles from everyone; at least, they cuddled a leg each. That was about as high as they could reach.

Meanwhile, Krysis threw a fatherly arm round Perilus. 'Well done, Perilus! You have saved the day,' Krysis said. 'Now we can get on and find the real thief. *Tempus fugit.*'

Ah, the old Latin again. Have we had that one yet? It means 'time flies'. In other words, time is rushing past and we had better get a move on before it leaves us all completely behind. Try it on your dad, as in, 'Come on, Dad! The match is about to start. *Tempus fugit!*' Your dad will think you're proper clever, and he'll be quite right too. Anyhow, it was nice to see and hear Krysis praising his son for once.

We had a right old party when we got back home. Since Krysis was sent to prison, we have been living in a very pokey, smelly and dirty apartment while that pompous ass called Fibbus Biggus is living in our lovely villa. Anyhow, the titchy apartment we have been forced to live in is above a couple I prefer to call The Ghastlies, also known as Crabbus and his wife, Septicaemia. They are a pain in the *culus*. (You can work that one out for yourself.)

They complained.

'Stop making that row up there!' they yelled in chorus.

'Stop shouting!' we shouted back.

'We'll call the guards and get you taken off to prison,' bellowed Crabbus.

'Just one problem,' I called back. 'The prison doesn't have gates any more. *Hurr hurr hurr!*'

'We'll get you in the end!' Crabbus roared. 'You pesky black chicken!'

Chicken? Me? I don't think so. Anyway, there was something much more interesting going on because Maddasbananus had just come whizzing into the courtyard at high speed and, quite unable to stop himself, had crashed headlong through Trendia's front window. (Good thing there wasn't any glass in it – just a bit of old cloth as a curtain.)

Maddasbananus is an inventor. So far he has invented a sewing machine (doesn't actually work), a time machine (doesn't work), a weaving machine (doesn't work) and a telephone (that doesn't work either). Success is not very familiar to poor young Maddasbananus.

However, the inventor has at least been successful in one venture. He has fallen in love. Oh yes, head over heels – in fact, head over heels and right through the window in this instance. *Hurr hurr hurr!* I should really be a comedian.

Fortunately for Maddasbananus, the object of his love, Trendia, has fallen head over heels in love with him too. Their world is full of twittering birds, fluffy rabbits, hearts beating as one and pretty flowers and all that sort of gooey stuff, again.

When Trendia, who was upstairs partying with the others, saw poor Maddasbananus crash through her window, she assumed the worst – she thought that he'd been killed. Trendia let out the most awful scream, 'Aaaaaaaaaaaaaaaaaargh!' (I told you it was most awful. Whaddya mean, you don't think that's an awful scream? You have to read it to yourself much louder, like

AAAAAAAAAAAARGH!

See, that's better, isn't it? Yes, it is. Stop saying, 'No, it isn't.' Listen, who's telling this story, you or me? NO, IT ISN'T YOU, NUTHEAD! Stop it and just read on. Thank you.)

Trendia went racing down the stairs three at a time (she's pretty nimble, that young woman),

hurled herself into her house and threw herself
at Maddasbananus, who was just struggling to
his feet and immediately got mown down by
Trendia, and then they both crashed to the floor.

'Are you hurt? Are you all right? Are you
breathing? Oh you poor lamb, my little chicken,
my delicious dormouse!'

Hang on! Maddasbananus can't be three
creatures at once, can he? Doesn't being a human
come into this at all? Not that Trendia cared,
because she was busy kissing him better. Oh dear,
I think we should leave them to it. So close your
eyes and let's just sing for a little bit. *Tra la la, dum
di dum, tiddly po, tiddly tum, fa la la la.* Oh good,
they've stopped. OK, you can open your eyes
now.

The thing is, how did Maddasbananus manage
to come whizzing into the courtyard so fast? Why
couldn't he stop? I will tell you. Maddasbananus
was busily demonstrating his latest invention: the
skateboard!

There! I bet you didn't know the Romans invented the skateboard, did you? Or at least one Roman (Maddasbananus) did. Wasn't he clever? Yes, he was. Give him a biscuit! **Kraaaarrkkk!**

3. Phew! Things Never Stop Happening, Do They?

'I'm going to sell my skateboard idea to the Roman Army,' declared Maddasbananus proudly. 'Just imagine whole legions of highly trained soldiers dashing into battle on skateboards. They will be invincible! And I shall be super-rich!' He beamed at Trendia, who blushed prettily and told Maddasbananus he was very clever, but if he could manage to get that sewing-machine idea working then she would be eternally grateful.

'Yes, yes,' Maddasbananus answered, 'but I have news, big news. Did you hear the Emperor's announcement?'

Everyone stopped and looked at the inventor.

'What announcement?' demanded Krysis.

'Actually, there are two announcements. They've been pinned up in the forum. First, Emperor Tyrannus has pardoned Scorcha.'

'Ah!' squeaked Hysteria, and she promptly fainted into her mother's arms. Flavia patted the girl's cheeks.

'Wakey-wakey, come on.'

Hysteria looked up into her mother's eyes. 'Is it true, Mater? Scorcha has been pardoned?'

'It would seem so, darling. Yes.'

'Aaaah!' Hysteria squeaked and fainted all over again.

Knowing Hysteria like I do, this could probably go on for ages so let's skip any more fainting and move on to the second announcement from Rome's great Emperor. Krysis demanded to know what it was.

Maddasbananus couldn't hide his excitement. 'Tyrannus has declared that there will be The Greatest Chariot Race On Earth, next week, at the Circus Maximus. Charioteers from across the Roman Empire are invited to take part so that we can find one great winner – the Chariot Champion of the Roman Empire!'

'Wow!' breathed Perilus, his eyes shining like a pair of comets. 'I wish I could take part!'

A hard frown descended on Krysis's face. 'Perilus! Remember, you are a high-born Roman, not some slave-cum-charioteer like Scorcha. Boys with your high background do not go charioteering.'

'I like charioteering and Scorcha is an *ex*-slave, Pater,' Perilus reminded his father. 'Now he's in the Green Team and he's their best rider. He's taught me how to be a charioteer too.'

Krysis ground his teeth. 'Yes, he did and I wish he hadn't. You get into enough dangerous scrapes as it is without throwing yourself in front of galloping horses and chariot wheels. You can barely put on your own sandals without hurting yourself. When will you learn that you are quite simply accident-prone? The main reason I don't want you charioteering is that I don't want to see you carted off in a coffin. Charioteering is very, VERY dangerous.'

Er-hrrrrm. (Clearing my throat again to get attention.) Krysis doesn't know that Perilus has already been charioteering. In fact, Scorcha only got into the famous Green Team because Perilus took his place in a race and won it for him! The boy actually won! He was brilliant. Krysis would go crazy if he knew about it. Poor Perilus, eh?

Anyhow, what excitement! Just to add to it all, Scorcha himself came wandering in. You

could see from the mile-wide smile on his face
that he had heard the news − a pardon and an
amazing chariot race coming up and, and, and,
AND standing there in front of him was the
beautiful, beaming Hysteria, her eyes shining
with adoration. Shall we close our own eyes and
do some more *tra la la*-ing? No, we shan't because
here is Krysis, with another severe frown crashing
down upon his face.

'Don't look at that young man with those doe
eyes, child!' roared Krysis. 'We have a visitor
coming to see you. I have arranged for Fibbus
Biggus to come and court you and ask for your
hand in marriage!'

'Fibbus Biggus!' cried Scorcha, suddenly
drowning in despair. (Splash!)

'Fibbus Biggus!' wailed Hysteria. Then
guess what? Yes, you're absolutely right. She
fainted again and sank to the floor with a rather
satisfying *fflurrppp* noise. (That was because Flavia
failed to catch her this time.)

Perilus glared at his father. 'Pater! You cannot force Hysteria to marry a hundred-year-old, fat, stupid bank manager and you can't stop me from being a charioteer either.'

Oh dear! Brave words from a foolish boy. I know Perilus is only eleven and I know how deeply he feels about these things but there is a time and a place for such discussions and this wasn't the time or the place. To be fair, I'm not sure when the time would be right or where the

right place was, but it certainly wasn't now. Krysis
was like a pot on a roaring fire – about to boil
over – and boil over he did.

Hysteria was sent to her room. Perilus
was sent to his room. Scorcha, Trendia and
Maddasbananus were sent home (in other words,
downstairs) and that was the end of the party.

Krysis even told me to go and stick my beak
in my nest, which I thought was very unkind of
him, especially as he didn't say 'beak'; he called
it a 'hooter'. There! My magnificent beak. It's
a whopper. It's a corker. But it's not a 'hooter'.
That's just rude. I do have some pride but, as
you well know, I am never one to boast. *Corvus
maximus intelligentissimusimusimusimus.* That's me,
plain and simple. Give us a biscuit!

So that left Tiddles and me out in the
courtyard all on our own, apart from Putuponn,
The Ghastlies' little slave. She was busily hanging
out their washing, again. Honestly, that poor girl
doesn't do anything else. Putuponn is a twenty-

four-hour laundry on legs. It's just washing, washing, washing all day long and the courtyard is never empty of sheets galore.

Tiddles and I were just having a nice, quiet chat about this when I heard the distinct sound of marching feet approaching. *Trudge trudge trudge trudge.* I could also hear the sound of voices, rather familiar voices. It was Plausible and the prison guards.

I quickly shoved Tiddles behind all the sheets. Well, I didn't exactly shove her because a raven shoving an elephant would be a bit like you trying to shove – well, an elephant, and elephants can't be shoved anywhere. No, what I did was to encourage her with wise words, like: 'Quick, Tiddles, get your *culus* behind those sheets before those guards can see you!'

It was all done in the nick of time. No sooner was Tiddles behind the sheets than the guards came marching into the courtyard.

'Halt!' yelled Plausible. The four of them

stopped and began peering round. Plausible soon spotted Putuponn and me.

'We are looking for an elephant,' said Plausible. 'Have you seen one?'

'What? Who? Us? An elephant? An elephant here? Don't be ridiculous.'

'Don't start that again! My name is Plausible. That guard there is Ridiculus!'

I raised one wing rather casually and sniffed my wing-pit as if I wasn't the least bit interested in guards or elephants.

Plausible's eyes narrowed. 'An elephant smashed down the prison gates and we must arrest her.' Plausible took several steps closer, bent down and eyeballed me.

'The elephant,' he went on, 'was last seen in the company of a talking raven.'

'Really?' I answered calmly.

'Yes,' put in Ludicrus. 'And he looked just like you and he talked just like you.'

'He might have looked like me, but he

certainly couldn't talk like me because no bird, NO BIRD, is as good at talkin' as I am. Besides, I am not a raven. I'm a robin.'

'Robin!' scoffed Ridiculus. 'Robins are small and have red breasts.'

'You are absolutely correct,' I said. 'You are, of course, referrin' to the common or garden robin redbreast. I, on the other hand, or should I say on the other wing, *hurr hurr hurr*, am a Lesser Sooty Robin.'

The four guards stared at me. 'By Jupiter,'

breathed Namelus. 'I have never in my whole life seen a Lesser Sooty Robin. But you're enormous. Do you mean to say that there is a GREATER Sooty Robin, even bigger than you?'

'Oh yes, and it is truly gigantic, as big as an elephant. Now, if you wouldn't mind —'

At that moment a terribly loud, elephantine rumbling noise drifted out from amongst the sheets.

SPRRRRRRRRRRPPPPP!

'Jupiter's underpants! What was that?' yelled Plausible, leaping backwards.

Putuponn placed a dainty hand over her mouth. 'I'm terribly sorry,' she murmured shyly. 'It was my lunch repeating.'

Plausible wiped his brow. 'Phew! That's a relief. Right, men, we go. Keep your eyes peeled for an escaped elephant. We'll find it sooner or later! Quick march!'

The guards disappeared round the corner. I waited until they had gone and then turned to Putuponn.

'Thank you so much, my dear,' I said. 'That was most timely and helpful of you. Tiddles! You can come out now.'

There was a rustle and a bustle and Tiddles reappeared, looking rather sheepish. Can an elephant look sheepish? Can a sheep look elephantish? Do we care? No, we don't. The guards had gone and that was a Good Thing. Let's all have a biscuit, and a special big one for

Putuponn, who might be a slave but she is kind
and quick-thinking and so much more. Biscuits
all round!

BUT – first there was work to be done.
Crabbus and Septicaemia, better known as The
Ghastlies, would be back at any moment. We had
to get Tiddles away from the courtyard as quickly
as possible and without being seen by The
Ghastlies or the prison guards. It's all go, go, go!

4. One in a Million?

I whisked myself up to Perilus's room and perched on the window ledge. 'Perilus! We need you. We've got to get Tiddles away from here.'

Perilus was sitting on the floor. There weren't any chairs in the room, or cupboards, or beds for that matter. Everything had been left at the villa when the family was thrown out. Now the villa was home to Fibbus Biggus, who used to be Krysis's deputy at the Imperial Mint, where all the money in Rome is made.

Perilus gave me a doleful look. 'Can't you see I'm shut in my room?' He gave a long sigh. This was most unlike the young hothead I knew so well.

'Perilus, stop feeling sorry for yourself. We've got to hide Tiddles before The Ghastlies get back

or we shall all be back in jail before you can say,
"I arrest you for usin' an elephant to vandalize
public property, specifically the Imperial Prison,
and for aidin' and abettin' said elephant to
escape. Put on these manacles."'

'Not funny,' muttered Perilus.

'It's not meant to be funny,' I told him. 'We
must get Tiddles away, so kindly get up from
the filthy floor and get yourself over here by the
window.'

'I can't climb out of that, Croakbag! It's too
far down!'

'Just sit on the edge for a moment.'

You see, I don't simply have a big beak; I
have a big brain as well. I went and perched on
Tiddles's head and guided her over to Perilus's
window, where Tiddles wrapped her trunk round
the boy and lifted him on to her back.

'Now take Tiddles off to those woods and hide
her. I've got some important business with the
Emperor himself.'

I waited until I had seen Tiddles and Perilus safely turn the corner and vanish from sight. It wasn't a moment too soon. Crabbus and Septicaemia arrived back at the house.

'It's that wretched black bird,' hissed Crabbus as he walked into the courtyard. 'Always around, making trouble.'

'*YYYURRRKKK!*' screamed Septicaemia.

'Now what?' demanded Crabbus.

'I have just stepped in something absolutely filthy.' She came hopping out from behind one of the sheets. Her left foot was plastered with steaming muck.

Ah! So that's what happened when Tiddles made that awful noise. Oh well, that's Nature, I suppose.

Septicaemia fixed me with a glare. 'YOU did this, you disgusting creature!'

Well, I was almost speechless for at least five seconds while I gathered my thoughts. How could Septicaemia possibly think I had made that . . . pile?

'My dear lady,' I began, because it's always wise to start a conversation politely. 'My dear lady, if you could just for a few moments manage to put into use what little brain you have, you would realize that a heap of manure that large could not possibly have come from a small creature such as myself. I could, if you wish, go into biological and anatomical detail and explain the impossibility of such an occurrence, but I fear your cranial capacity would go into overload and quite possibly explode.'

There! You see what a master of words I am. Have you ever known a raven like it? Of course not. I am *Corvus superbus*, *Corvus extraordinarium*, *Corvus supremus*!

Sadly, my words didn't seem to touch Septicaemia or her husband. She looked at Crabbus in what can only be described as stupefaction.

'What is that bird gibbering about now?' she demanded to know.

'I'm not at all sure,' sneered Crabbus, 'but it sounded to me as if he was being deliberately rude about you.'

Ah! Dear Crabbus! Such a bright fellow, I don't think. But it was high time for me to leave. There were important things to be done. Did I say I had to see the Emperor? I did. So off I went.

It's hard being a talking bird in a world of humans. They all think they are so very important – by far the most important creatures on earth. But I have one simple question to ask.

Can humans fly? The answer, naturally, is NO. They can walk and run. They can speak. They can even think; at least they call it thinking. But can they lift their arms, catch the wind then simply lift off the ground and float upwards into the blue beyond? Can they soar and glide? Can they swoop and dive and hover in mid-air? Of course they can't, and yet they believe themselves to be superior to all other creatures.

So there I was, flying high above the greatest city on earth.

Whaddya mean, New York? What are you on about? I'm talking about Rome! Just when I was beginning to think you were clever, you go and make comments like that. New York? I've never even heard of it.

Anyhow, back to the old flying business. I was flipping and flapping my way over the forum to the Emperor's palace. I had decided it was time to pay a call on Tyrannus, Emperor of Rome and most of the world beyond.

I found him in the palace garden, feeding the fish in the big pond. Actually, he was feeding the big fish *with* little fish, chucking in goldfish for the pike to eat. That's emperors for you – addicted to casual violence. Always best to keep on the right side of them, if you ask me.

'*Salve*, Tyrannus!' I crawked. The Emperor looked up and gave me a curt nod.

'Ah, it's the black rascal himself,' drawled Tyrannus. 'What do you want, Croakbag? You do want something, don't you? I only ever see you when you want something from me.'

I ignored his little jibes. I have my self-respect, you see!

'As a matter of fact, I have come to see how well you did at the chariot races. Did you take my tip? Did you put money on Scorcha to win?'

'Yes, and did I not fulfil my promise and pardon the lad? He rode well. In fact, he rode so well that I came up with the idea of a chariot competition. You heard the announcement?'

I congratulated him.
'Everyone is talkin' about it,
Tyrannus. Great idea.'

Tyrannus smiled. The
Emperor has a peculiar smile. It's a
sort of half-grin, half-snapping-of-teeth kind of
affair, as if he's about to chew your hand or bite
off your ear.

'I shall put money on Scorcha to win
the championship, but if he doesn't
I might have to throw him to the
lions.' As he spoke, Tyrannus
chucked another couple
of goldfish to the
gaping mouth of
the pike in
the pond.

The Emperor turned back to me and fixed me with glittering eyes.

'You've been making mischief, I hear,' he said.

'Really? Me? You can't trust gossip. You should know that, bein' Emperor. The palace is full of whispers, and most of them spun from nothin'.'

'True, true,' nodded Tyrannus. 'But, on the other hand, prison gates being busted open by elephants is a bit more noticeable than a whisper, don't you think?'

'Ah,' I murmured. And I would probably have turned red with embarrassment if I wasn't already black. 'But those brainless guards of yours had put Krysis back in jail. How is he to find the real thief – the man who stole 10,000 silver denarii from you – if he's in jail?'

'You might have a point there,' agreed Tyrannus. 'But this is your last chance, or rather it is Krysis's last chance. The thief must be found or I shall have to banish Krysis and his family from the country and he will never get his home back.' A few more goldfish went to the pike. 'So, my dear crow −'

'Raven,' I corrected, but Tyrannus ignored me. He's like that. It's deliberate. He's the Emperor.

'My dear crow,' he repeated. 'You have two messages to take back to your friends from me. Scorcha is the man! But will he be the man at the end of the greatest charioteer competition? If he isn't, it might well be feeding time for the lions at the Colosseum. And then there's Krysis and the thief. Get it sorted, you black-feathered wretch!'

Tyrannus turned his back on me and strode to the palace. I watched him uneasily as he climbed the steps up to the doors and disappeared inside. He had made it quite clear that *tempus* was *fugit-*ing very fast indeed.

I needed to think of some way to speed up the investigation. Now, you know that I don't like to boast but −

Whaddya mean, interrupting me like this?

I DO like to boast? Really? Is that what you think? Well, maybe I do, but IF I do, and it's a very big **IF**, if you ask me – IF I do boast, it's because I am making a true statement about myself. I can't help it if I'm clever. I can't help it if I have to solve half of Rome's problems. And I can't help it if I get really good ideas like the one I have just had about Krysis and the real thief.

My amazing brain had just remembered something that could be very useful. Take your mind back to when Tiddles broke open the prison gates. Try to remember the escaping prisoners and one prisoner in particular, a prisoner with sticking-out ears and a long nose. I bet you can't recall his name, can you? No, I thought so. Well, you see, I can. I remember. Am I not the brainiest raven of them all, Croakbag, *Corvus mega-maximus biggus bonsus*? The prisoner's name was Blabbus. He had told me several times that you 'hear all sorts of stuff in prison'. And Blabbus had looked straight at Krysis. Now why would Blabbus do that unless he was trying to tell me something about Krysis?

And this is where I blame myself. I was too caught up with the escape to realize it at the time. I just hoped that it wasn't too late now. I had to find Blabbus. There was just one problem. There are almost a million people living in Rome, and all I had to do was find one of them. One in a million? **Kraaarrrkkk!**

5. The Lunatic Professor Gets Lucky!

Blabbus has a face like an elephant. He could have been Tiddles's little brother. I'm joking, of course. Anyhow, the fact that he had a face like an elephant didn't make it any easier to track him down.

I perched myself on top of the Emperor's palace, overlooking the forum. They say that if you stand in the forum long enough you'll see everyone you know. In other words, sooner or later Blabbus was bound to turn up. But the thing is, how long do you have to wait? A few minutes? An hour? A day? A month? Several bloomin' years! By Jupiter, I couldn't just hang around and hope.

Then *ker-ping!* A little idea popped into my big black noddle. Oh yes! I opened my flappers and

swooped like a shadow down
to the forum and parked my
bum on Caesar's head. (It was
his statue, not the real Caesar.
I'm not stupid.) I perched there,
sharpened my beady eyes and
began looking round. The place
was crowded – people out doing
their shopping, having a natter
with friends and so on. Perfect.
There's nothing like a big, noisy
crowd to attract your low-down
criminal, such as pickpockets
and shoplifters.

It didn't take me long to spot a pickpocket at work. She was just a kid and couldn't have been more than eleven or twelve. There's usually a gang of them working for a master. I needed to get to her before she disappeared in the crowd. I followed her out of the forum and watched as she climbed up the hill and headed out to the dirty suburbs. When she stopped for a short rest and to inspect her booty I casually dropped down beside her.

'Mornin'!' I greeted her and she almost died on the spot. I love it when they get the frights like that.

'Jupiter's underpants!' she squeaked. 'It's a talkin' bird!'

'Croakbag, real name *Corvus maximus just-about-everythingus*. Pleased to meet you. Been havin' a good day?'

The girl grabbed her little bag of swag and pulled it closer to her chest. 'What do you mean?' she asked. See? She was suspicious and a bit scared, and that was good. That meant she was more likely to be helpful.

'Oh nothin' much. Just that I was watchin'. Amazin' what you can see when you're watchin'. I was down in the forum an' I saw you there an' I thought to myself: *She's a clever little minx. I bet she knows lots.*'

'I wasn't doin' nothin'!' she squawked.

Er-hrrrm hrrrm – that's me clearing my throat again. I can't bear misuse of language. Time for a little lesson.

'I'm afraid that's what we call a double negative, Miss,' I pointed out. 'An' that's somethin' that's not allowed. You can't say, "I wasn't doin' nothin'". You see, "wasn't" is negative and so is "nothin'". So you end up contradicting yourself because if you wasn't doin' nothin' you must have been doin' somethin'. QED. And that is Latin for *quod erat demonstrandum*, which means "I have just proved what I said was true". What you can say is "I was doin' nothin'" or "I wasn't doin' anythin'". Do you see?'

I looked at her and I can only say that she was looking back at me as if I was some kind of lunatic professor.

'What are you?' she demanded. 'Are you some kind of lunatic professor?' (See? Told you so.)

I sighed and decided to give up my little grammar lesson even though I thought it very kind of me to have gone to so much trouble. I mean, you understand, don't you? You know what I was getting at. Of course you do, because you are super-intelligent, like me, but obviously not quite as super as me because, well, nobody, but NOBODY is as clever as Croakbag. **Kraaarrkk!** Give us a biscuit!

'OK, forget it,' I prattled on. 'Just tell me somethin'. Have you ever seen a man with a face like an elephant?'

'Is this a joke?' asked the girl. 'I mean, is it like when you say, "What do you call a man with a face like an elephant?" And I say, "I don't know. What DO you call a man with a face like an elephant?" Then you say something funny, like, er, "Trunky" or "Ellyface".'

It was my turn to look at the girl as if *she* was crazy. I shook my feathers and tried to push my brain back into a place where common sense lived.

'It's not a joke. All I want to know is this: do you know a man with a face like an elephant – big, long nose and sticking-out ears?'

'What if I do? Nothin' wrong with that. Anyway, why should I tell you?'

'Because you are a common criminal,' I pointed out. 'You're a pickpocket. I saw you. But don't worry. I'm not tellin'. I just want an answer to the question.'

'Promise you won't tell.'

'I promise.'

'Cross your heart and hope to die?'

'I cross my heart.'

'Cross your legs, turn round three times and say, "Rumble bumble, jellyfish and jumble, beat me with a pudding spoon and stuff me in the crumble."'

'Don't be silly,' I said, shaking my head. 'Just get on with it and answer the question.'

'Yes,' she said.

Aha! Things were looking up. 'What's his name?'

'Bliblib? Blobalob? Blubberlub?'

'Blabbus?' I suggested. She nodded! THE GIRL NODDED! She KNEW! My heart was starting to race.

'OK,' I said. 'Now, think. Where will I find him?'

'Don't know,' she said, and her eyes took on a vacant look.

'Yes, you do! Think! Where?'

She suddenly jerked into life again. 'Oh yeah! He's in prison!'

'No, he isn't. He escaped.' I looked at her carefully. I was sure she knew. She was hiding something. Time to put on more pressure.

'You know I promised not to tell anyone?'

'Yeah?'

I smiled. Not that she could tell. I mean, I'm a bird. How do you tell when a bird's smiling? Not easy, is it?

'I've changed my mind,' I told the girl. 'I might have to tell someone after all.'

The girl looked at me and I gave her my steeliest, hardest stare back, so she knew I wasn't kidding.

'Where is Blabbus?' I repeated.

'He's my boss. I'm taking the stuff to him now.'

Praise be to Jupiter! It couldn't get any better. The poor creature was going to take me right to Blabbus himself.

So off we went and it wasn't very far. Now then, prepare yourself for a shock. You probably think of ancient Rome as a great, glorious, glittering city, full of painted statues, some of them even decorated with gold. There are shining temples all over the place and smart people in wonderful togas and soldiers in sparkly uniforms and fabulous villas with underfloor heating and mosaics and fountains and all that Roman stuff. And then there's the Rome I was in now, led there by this young slip of a thing. It was dirty. It was dusty and musty. It was full of the thinnest, most skeletal dogs you have ever seen, prowling the piles and piles of rubbish for

food. There were scrawny kids playing in the streets, beggars everywhere, filthy tumbledown shacks and Blabbus was in one of them. He was surrounded by some of his little thieves; they were all kids, of course.

As we pushed away the torn and tattered rags that were supposed to be the front door, Blabbus looked up. His eyes lit on me and he smiled and roared.

'Welcome! I knew you'd turn up sooner or later!'

'Blabbus,' I said. 'Nice place you have here.'

Blabbus burst out laughing. 'I like a crow with a sense of humour.'

'Raven,' I corrected. 'Crows are smaller. And you can call me Croakbag.'

Blabbus looked me up and down. 'So,' he said. 'What do you want to know?'

'You said you knew somethin' about my master, Krysis. I want to know what it is.'

'Information is expensive,' said Blabbus. 'And it don't look to me as if you've got any money on you.'

'Freedom is even more expensive,' I pointed out. 'And you've escaped from prison and I know where you are.' I paused to let this sink in and quietly added, 'I might tell someone. Oh dear. What a disaster that might be.'

Blabbus stepped

closer and we eyeballed each other for at least fifteen seconds. (That's a long time if you're eyeballing someone.)

'I could wring your neck,' hissed Blabbus.

'You'd have to catch me first.'

We did ten more seconds of eyeballing. Blabbus relaxed.

'OK. Since it was because of your master that I was able to escape prison, I guess I owe him a favour. While we were all in prison together, a visitor arrived. The visitor had come to see one of the guards, Ludicrus. I happened to overhear their conversation and it was all about money they had stolen from the Imperial Mint.' Blabbus looked at me.

At last the truth was about to be divulged! I edged a little closer. 'You know who took it?'

Blabbus nodded. 'I know who took it and I know who put it in

Krysis's villa. You see, there were two of them, working together.'

'Who?'

Blabbus leaned forward with a smile. He told me. My heart soared.

Krraaarrrkkkkk! Give the man a biscuit – the biggest and best one you've got!

6. The Goat is Redundant

I am the raven! Did I flap back to my lovely
Roman family? Did I fly? No. I FLOATED!
I floated and soared and drifted like a dove
stretching out on a soft bed made from clouds of
love. Ahhh! You can probably tell I was happy. I
was on my way home to spill the great news to
Krysis and his suffering family. In a few seconds I
would be able to tell them who had stolen – Ah!
But wait, wait! No, I couldn't. I couldn't tell them
yet because the most enormous brainwave I had
ever had almost made me fly straight into a tree.

OK, I know I'm clever. People are always
telling me. Well, maybe it's mostly me telling
myself but nevertheless it is true. I am BRAINY!
Even so, having said that, I surprise myself
sometimes by the sheer genius of my plans,

and the one that had me nearly parking my whopper of a beak in a sudden tree that wasn't there moments before was a plan of not just genius, but G.E.N.I.U.S, in capital letters with rockets shooting out at all angles and little twinkly stars going off and everyone shouting, 'Hurrah for Croakbag, *Corvus mega-brilliantissimussimussimussimuss*!' Oh yes.

The only slightly annoying thing about my plan was that I would have to sit on it for the time being and it's very difficult to sit on something you know when it is so sparkly and humungously important and you want to tell the Whole World. But that is what I had to do and that is what I did.

It was just as well that when I did eventually float down to the old house and home there was lots going on. Maddasbananus and Trendia had just announced their wedding. They had! Hearts and flowers and kisses and cuddles and all that gooey, lovey-dovey-I-don't-know-what

kind of stuff going on. Flavia had baked a
special pizza-cake to celebrate and Trendia and
Maddasbananus were going around with mile-
wide smiles. I've never seen so many teeth on
display at the same time. **Kraarrkkk! Toc-
toc-toc!**

Flavia has got her hands full at the moment because she's baking like crazy, getting ready for the Greatest Charioteer competition. I might add that Perilus and Scorcha are getting ready too. I saw them out at the back, practising with Trendia's goat.

They had harnessed the horned and hairy beast to a little chariot and were racing up and down behind the house. Good thing Krysis couldn't see them or he would have had a, well, a crisis. He doesn't like Perilus doing any chariot racing.

But Perilus is Perilus and Danger is his middle name. (Not really, it's actually Marcus.) Now there's a lad who loves to feel his heart pumping wildly in his chest. How many times have I seen him balancing on a rope stretched between two trees? Dozens of times. How many times have I seen him fall off? Dozens. But does that stop him? No, it doesn't. He was born for danger.

So, things are getting hot, especially Flavia's stove. *Hurr hurr hurr*, raven joke! I don't half crack them! I told a joke to a pal of mine recently and he couldn't stop laughing. Laughed so hard he fell out of his tree. He lay on the ground squawking helplessly, looked up at me and said, 'You're ravin'!' And quick as a flash I opened my wings wide and said, 'I know I'm a raven!' Then we both fell about all over again.

Whaddya mean, it's not THAT funny? Show me a bird that tells better jokes than me. Go on, show me. See, you can't, can you? Get back in your cupboard and stop interrupting.

Anyhow, it's busy, busy, busy. Scorcha practising for the competition; Flavia, Fussia and Hysteria having races of their own round the kitchen, making pizzas; Krysis getting ready to marry off his only daughter to Fibbus Biggus, and Maddasbananus showing Trendia his latest invention.

Now, if there's anyone in Rome who can come up with ideas that are almost as brilliant as mine, it is Maddasbananus. It's not his fault if most of his inventions don't work. Hmmm, actually it might be his fault. But, anyway, the important thing is to HAVE IDEAS in the first place. Where are we without ideas? In the dark, that's where. Then someone invents the oil lamp and . . . whoopee! Light in the darkness. See? That's how important having ideas is.

Maddasbananus had been working on his latest idea: the spin drier. He had already tried a first version. It looked like a horizontal windmill. You stuck the clothes on the whirly bit. Beneath

that were lots of cogs and wheels and a pole
sticking out. Trendia's goat was tied to the pole.
When the goat began to walk round and round,
the clothes started spinning faster and faster
until most of them fell off and immediately got
trodden into the dirt by the goat. So much for the
Spin Drier, Mark I.

Now it was time for the Spin Drier, Mark II.
(That's 'two' in Roman times. You know all about
Roman counting, don't you? If you're stuck, ask
your mum or dad. See how much THEY know!
You might catch them out. *Hurr hurr hurr!*)

Maddasbananus had come up with an
adaptation. He had decided that the bit that
went wrong was the goat. A goat was too fast
and strong. On the other hand, he couldn't think
what to use in place of the goat to power the
spin drier. Then, a couple of mornings ago, he
had been watching Putuponn, The Ghastlies'
slave, hanging out the washing, AGAIN! And he
noticed the wind making the sheets flap about all

over the place. It was almost as if the sheets were trying to run away. You could almost hear them shouting: 'STOP WASHING US! WE ARE FED UP WITH ALL THE WASHING WE ARE GETTING! PICK ON SOMETHING YOUR OWN SIZE AND SHAPE. JUST LEAVE US ALONE!'

Maddasbananus was watching all this and PING! Do you know what came into his head? The wind. And I don't mean the wind blew in through one earhole and out through the other. The wind went in and stirred things up in that funny noddle of his. He ran into his inventing room and got stuck in.

Now look at him! Here he is, proudly showing Trendia the Spin Drier, Mark II. It was made mostly from wood. At the bottom was a large, square box with the same old cogs and wheels inside. A tall pole stuck up from the centre. The pole had six wooden spokes sticking out horizontally. Maddasbananus had threaded some thin rope through the spokes so that the rope spiralled out from the centre and went round and round through each spoke in turn until it reached the outer edge, and there it stopped.

'But where's the goat?' asked Trendia, who was looking rather doubtful about the new project.

Maddasbananus beamed at his wife-to-be. 'All you need is a little bit of wind. It only starts working when you put some clothes on it. Try.'

'But I haven't done any washing,' Trendia giggled.

'Doesn't matter. Put some dry clothes on it.'

Trendia fetched some clothes and hung them on the spiralling line. The wind gently blew and the clothes began to flap and try to run away. Then the wooden cogs began to creak and squeak and slowly the wind started to push the flapping clothes round and round.

Everyone stared.

'By Jupiter, it works!' whispered Krysis in astonishment.

'It works!' cried Trendia, throwing her arms round Maddasbananus and kissing him. (He was her almost-husband after all, so kissing was allowed.)

'It works!' murmured Maddasbananus, his eyes almost tearful. At last he had invented something that really, really worked.

I have to say, I was overcome. I had tears in my own eyes. I flapped down and landed on the inventor's shoulder. 'Brilliant,' I told him. 'It's utterly brilliant. I couldn't have made it better myself.'

Trendia looked at me sharply. 'Croakbag, you couldn't have made it AT ALL! You're a bird!'

'Beggin' your pardon, Trendia, I am not simply "a bird". I am *Corvus* –'

'Not another word,' said Trendia, and the woman grabbed my hooter and shut it with a noisy *clack*. 'I'm tired of your boasting. This is Maddasbananus's day, not yours. You, dear Croakbag, are A BIRD and Maddasbananus is my genius husband-to-be and he is AMAZING!'

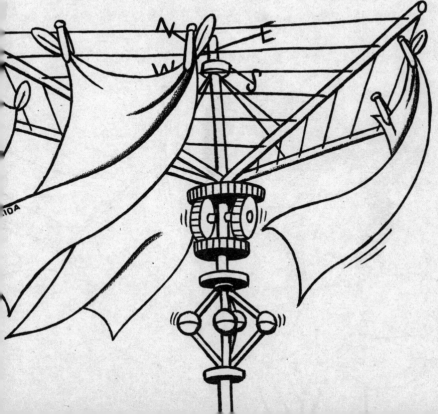

At that point she let go of my beak and I sighed deeply. I suppose she was right. (Apart from the bit about me being just 'a bird'.) It was Maddasbananus's day, and hers. Two young lovers! What could I do except say **Kraaarrkk!** Give 'em both a heart-shaped biscuit!

7. A Wedding

The wedding took place that very afternoon.
Trendia's parents were no longer alive, having
been buried under several tons of ash when
Vesuvius erupted and smothered Pompeii.

You could say that poor Trendia had been
rather unlucky. Her first husband had been a
soldier and had died on the end of someone's
sword in some pointless battle. That is to say the
battle was pointless but, unfortunately, the sword
wasn't. In fact, the sword had a very sharp point
and had made a point of making a point. *Hurr
hurr hurr!*

Then her mum and dad get clobbered by a
whopping great volcano. It was lucky Trendia
wasn't there or she'd have got clobbered too. She
had only just left Pompeii to seek her fortune in

Rome. I think she's still looking for that fortune but at least she has found love once more in the arms of Maddasbananus, as good a man as there can be.

The priest arrived. He was a funny-looking chap, by the name of Myopia. He was tall and scrawny and looked a bit like a wet dishcloth after you've wrung it and squeezed out as much water as you can. His long, thin, grey hair was tied in a ponytail and reached right down his back. It hung there looking so, SO tempting, as if it was inviting you to give it a great big tug.

So I did. You should have heard him squawk!

SKRAAARRRRKKKKK!

And he jumped too! Both feet off the ground at the same time!

'Croakbag!' cried Flavia. 'Why did you do that?'

'I was just wonderin' if perhaps it was real, an' it is. Pardon me for botherin' and hope I didn't cause any inconvenience.'

'Inconvenience!' squeaked Myopia. He
had a very high, thin voice, like a whistle.
'Inconvenience! You almost pulled my head off!'

'Good thing I didn't then,' I retorted. 'Because
I could have. I pulled a head off a dead squirrel
the other day. Then I ate it.'

'I,' declared Myopia, pulling himself completely upright and banging his head on the ceiling as a result, 'am a PRIEST, not a squirrel.'

Myopia and I eyeballed each other for a few moments and then the priest asked who was going to give away the bride. Ah, you see, bit of a problem. That's the parents' job and they were rather indisposed beneath a large chunk of Vesuvius.

Flavia stepped forward and took Trendia by both hands. 'Krysis and I would be honoured to give you away and act as your parents, if you will allow us.'

Trendia threw both her arms round Flavia and hugged her. 'Thank you!' she gasped. 'You are so kind.' She glanced at Maddasbananus and he smiled and nodded, so that was all sorted. Flavia got hold of a white belt to tie round Trendia's waist. She tied it with the Knot of Hercules. That's a special knot the bride always has on her belt. Only her husband is allowed to untie it.

Whaddya mean, why is it called the Knot of Hercules? Because it was named after Hercules and don't ask me why he went round naming knots after himself. Everyone has to have a hobby. Maybe knot-naming was his. Now listen, there's a wedding going on, if you don't mind.

The priest did all his priestly things, incantations, mutterings, dropping things on the floor. (That was accidental, not part of the marriage service. He was a bit of a butterfingers.) Then a special offering was made to Jupiter to bless the marriage. (The offering was a pizza which Flavia hastily rustled up.) The pizza smelled so good Myopia couldn't resist eating half of it before he eventually remembered he was supposed to give it to the bride and groom to eat.

Then Maddasbananus swept Trendia off her feet and carried her to his house. We were all shouting and cheering. Trendia was carrying a special, flaming torch so she could light a

ceremonial fire in Maddasbananus's house. The
inventor put Trendia back on her feet and she
bent down and lit the fire. Soon the logs were
crackling. The torch was blown out and Trendia
tossed it to the crowd of excited guests. It was all
part of the ceremony.

BUT – I could hardly believe it. I watched the
torch as it cartwheeled through the air and I saw
the dead embers start glowing, then suddenly
it was aflame again. It hit the top of the door
and the flames caught hold of the straw roof.
In a moment it was ABLAZE! Flames were
soon racing across the roof towards the other
rooms – Trendia's and ours and, of course, The
Ghastlies'.

By this time everyone was shouting and
screaming and rushing about, abandoning the
house to the mercies of the fire. Perilus grabbed
a bucket and ran round and round, looking
for water to put in it. Krysis and Myopia were
dancing about, trying to stamp on the flaming

bits of straw that had fallen to the ground.
Hysteria was, guess what? Sobbing. Goodness,
at least she might have cried over the flames and
helped put them out.

Looking inside the house, I could see
flaming timbers falling down from the ceiling
and crashing to the floor. That was when
Maddasbananus did the maddest thing ever. He
dashed back inside, jumping over the flames and
disappearing from view. All we could see was fire
and flames.

'My husband!' screamed Trendia. 'We've only
been married five seconds! You can't die now!
Somebody save my husband!'

But there was no way anyone was going to
try to get through those raging flames. Suddenly,
great sprays of water came shooting out of the
house, along with the flames. The water spray
became stronger and stronger. Krysis and the
priest were soaked to the skin. Hysteria was
pretty wet too but that was mostly her own tears.

And there, miraculously, was Maddasbananus!
He was holding a thick leather hose with one
hand and pumping at some kind of machine with
the other. Water was gushing from the hose and
putting out the flames.

'Someone help me with the pump!' he
yelled. Perilus dashed forward and took over the

pumping. Now it was easier for the inventor to direct the hose with both hands and, with much hissing and spitting from the blaze, he put out the flames. At last, the fire was no more. The ground was soaked. The house was soaked. We were soaked. We looked at Maddasbananus's house. It was a blackened wreck.

'Oh,' murmured Trendia, her voice desperately sad.

The priest was looking intently at the hose and pump. 'What is that?' he squeaked.

'I call it a fire engine,' Maddasbananus explained. 'I invented it last week. It's for putting out fires. You can see it's on wheels, which means you can pull it anywhere. In fact, I could build a bigger one and have horses pull it. All it needs is a source of water and then you pump and pump and the water is pushed out through the nozzle on the end of the hose.'

'Remarkable,' mused Myopia. 'You saved the houses next to yours. That's the trouble with Rome – all these wooden buildings and straw roofs. They catch fire so easily and then it spreads. Before you know it, half the city's burned down. You should show your contraption to the Emperor. We need to have your – what did you call it?'

'Fire engine,' replied Maddasbananus, grinning.

'We need your fire engines in every part of the city.' The priest turned to Trendia. 'You've got a very clever husband,' he told her.

'I've got a very clever wife, actually,' said Maddasbananus, slipping his arm round Trendia's waist.

'And that makes two! What a clever pair!' I croaked.

Myopia looked at me rather disdainfully. 'Who asked you, squirrel-gobbler?' He turned away. 'Well, I shall be going. May the blessing of Jupiter be upon you both – and don't forget to see the Emperor.'

The priest threw me one final, evil glance and left. Personally speaking, I didn't think throwing evil glances around was a very priestly kind of thing to do but I'll get over it.

Maddasbananus spent most of the rest of his wedding day going through the ruins of his house, rescuing whatever he could. Trendia helped by taking a stack of clothes, which were all filled with smoke and soot, and washing them. You can guess where she hung them to dry.

Whaddya mean, on her nose! Are you trying to be funny? Oh, you are? Well, all right, I'll give you that one. Very funny, but I'll have you know that Trendia has a rather cute nose. It's not too long, not too short and it has holes in the right places. She doesn't have flared sniffers like a horse or squashed, piggy nostrils. It's just an everyday kind of Roman nose.

It had been a long day and it wasn't the way the wedding should have ended. Nevertheless, I have to admit that Myopia the priest was right about the fire engine. Maddasbananus really should demonstrate it to the Emperor, but how was he supposed to do that? Set fire to the palace? That would certainly put some heat on the Emperor. *Hurr hurr hurr!* Get over it!

8. What's the Smelliest Stuff in the World?

The excitement! Rome's buzzing! The streets are crowded! People are pouring into the city to watch The Greatest Chariot Race On Earth. Noise! Cheering! And, best of all, rich pickings for a raven like me – all that food you humans drop all over the place. By Jupiter, you're messy eaters!

Luckily it's a pleasure for me to clean up behind you. A bit of bread here, a morsel of stuffed dormouse there, just as long as I don't have to stick my conk into that horrible stinky fish sauce you lot like to slap on everything. I mean, there is a limit to how much disgusting stuff I can take and that limit is reached when it comes to STINKY FISH SAUCE.

But just listen to those crowds! You can almost touch the excitement it's so real. Scorcha's like a cat on hot bricks, leaping about, eyes bulging, quivering with anticipation. Hysteria's trailing after him like a lost calf, fetching this and that for him and constantly asking if he's all right.

Huh! Scorcha's all right, all right, if you get my drift. He's so pumped with energy you'd think he'd zoom into the sky. He can't wait for the races. In fact, he and Perilus and the whole family have made their way to the Circus Maximus. The newly-weds, Trendia and Maddasbananus, have come along too. It seems like the whole world is heading for the Circus.

I left them there for a short while as I had a rather important visit to make. There was someone I wanted to see at the palace. You can guess who. Exactly! The Emperor himself, Tyrannus.

I found him back in his bath. I think he's got a bit obsessive about keeping clean. If you ask me, he can't stand the guilt of all that blood on his hands – the prisoners he's had executed, the rivals he's had poisoned, the Christians he's sent to the lions. It's a wonder he can sleep at night. Perhaps he doesn't.

'*Salve*, Tyrannus!' I squawked as I flew in through the bathroom window.

'It's that wretched black flappy thing,' grunted the Emperor. 'Do you have to barge in on my bath time? Has Krysis found the thief yet?'

'Ah, funny you should mention that. The case is almost solved. I just need a wee bit more patience from you, dear Emperor. In the meantime, are you goin' to bet on Scorcha at the Race of Champions?'

At that Tyrannus managed to crack a smile. 'I shall, Croakbag. The boy did well last time.

I made a small fortune. Of course,' he added, inspecting his fingernails, 'I do have a rather large fortune anyhow, but I have now added the small fortune to the large fortune and so I have an even larger fortune. Am I right to put money on Scorcha again?'

I cocked my head on one side. 'I would bet a dead cow on Scorcha, if I had a dead cow.'

Whaddya mean, that's disgusting? I'll tell you something, STINKY FISH SAUCE is disgusting! That's what! I don't know how these Romans eat it. Anyhow, I'm a raven. Do ravens have money? No, they don't. Money is of no interest to us. What do us birds value most of all? I will tell you. Food. FOOD. And for me a dead cow would be the greatest good fortune a raven could have. A whole dead cow all to myself! My beak is dribbling at the merest thought of it.

Tyrannus understood me at once and burst out laughing. 'A whole dead cow, eh, Croakbag, you rascal. You really think Scorcha is better than any other charioteer in the world?'

'I do.'

'I'll put money on him then.'

I nodded with satisfaction.

'Now get out of my bathroom and leave me in peace.'

'*Vale*, Tyrannus!'

'Just leave mc in peace, will you, you feathered bag of badness?'

I spread my flappers and winged it back to the Circus Maximus, where there seemed to be a bit of an uproar amongst the Green Team's camp. I swooped down and landed on Perilus's shoulder. The boy gasped, his face as grey as a bowl of stinky fish sauce.

'Croakbag! You've got to help!' Perilus cried. 'Scorcha's been kidnapped!'

I almost choked. 'Don't be silly. I left you only a few minutes ago and you were all together then. How come you let him be kidnapped?'

'We didn't. He went down to check the horses and he never came back.'

The leader of the Green Team, Primus, stepped forward. 'One of the slaves working in the stables says he saw Scorcha being hustled away by two burly figures in cloaks. The slave said he couldn't see their faces and it looked as if Scorcha was unconscious.'

'He's been nobbled,' I croaked. 'Somebody doesn't want him to win so they've nobbled him. Got him out of the way.'

'Exactly,' nodded Primus. 'There are five heats before the final race. Scorcha has been drawn to race in the second heat. The first heat —'

Primus was suddenly interrupted by a huge cheer from the crowd. He went on. 'The first heat is already under way. Scorcha is on next, but there is no Scorcha. We're out of it.'

At that very moment a rather plump figure stepped out of the shadows. 'I can race in his place,' said the plump figure. Guess who? Jellus. Jellus — the man who used to be captain of the Green Team but was replaced by Scorcha. It wouldn't surprise me if Jellus had arranged the kidnapping himself.

HANG ON A SECOND!!!!

I'll just run that past my brain again. It wouldn't surprise me if Jellus had arranged the kidnapping himself. Of course he had! I'd bet my dead cow on it. (Assuming I'd won the dead cow in the first place, and yes, I do realize there is no dead cow. It's a hypothetical dead cow, and if you don't know what 'hypothetical' means, ask your teacher. It will give her or him a good opportunity to show you how much they know. Or not. *Toc-toc-toc!*)

The rest of the Green Team simply stared at Jellus and then at each other. What were they to do? None of them liked Jellus. He used to be a fast rider but now he was rather overweight. Nothing wrong with that, you might say, unless of course we're talking about riding horses and chariots and winning races. You don't want to carry extra weight. Weight slows things down.

'You need me,' said Jellus, standing there with his arms folded across his chest and looking all pompous and proud. Talk about a big-head. Actually, he was a big-stomach too. *Hurr hurr hurr!*

'I can do it!' said another, much smaller, quieter voice.

Huh? Who was that? Well, bless my beak and scrunch my eyes – it was Perilus!

Every single person turned and goggled at the boy. (MY boy! My Perilus, the daredevil!)

Krysis was the first to speak. 'Don't be daft,' he snapped.

Perilus stood his ground. 'I've done it before.'

Krysis burst out laughing. 'Racing goats round a courtyard is nothing like a real chariot race,' he pointed out.

Flavia smiled warmly at her son. 'Really, darling. It's lovely that you want to help but this is really grown-up stuff. Your father's right.'

'But he isn't,' said Perilus. 'That's just the thing! I *have* done it before.' Perilus turned to Primus. 'You remember when Scorcha first joined the Green Team? It was his first chariot race, and he won? That wasn't Scorcha, though he would have won anyway if it had been. He would have been much better than me. But I won that race. Scorcha was in prison and I couldn't let him miss his first test with the Green Team so I put on his helmet and took his place and I won. And after the race –'

Primus leaped forward and finished off. 'After the race you wouldn't take off your helmet when everyone was cheering you and shouting "Scorcha! Scorcha!" You wouldn't take off your helmet, which was too big for you anyway, because you didn't want to be recognized. By Jupiter, it was a boy!'

Primus turned in amazement and looked at the others. 'If Perilus did it once before maybe he can do it again.'

Jellus gave a roar of laughter. 'A boy! He's eleven! What does he know about racing against real opponents? Nothing. He has no experience, just one race when he was very lucky. I demand that I ride in the next heat!'

Primus nodded. 'Say what you like, Jellus. You're overweight and over the hill. The boy rides in the heat. Hurry, men, get him dressed. Give him a decent-sized helmet this time.'

Flavia rushed forward and clutched at Perilus. 'He can't ride! He could get killed! Maimed for life! What if he's shipwrecked?'

'I refuse to let him ride,' said Krysis, stepping forward and sticking out his chin as if his chin was in command of the world. 'I refuse. He's not riding.'

Hysteria suddenly burst into tears. I thought maybe she was upset at the idea of Perilus being shipwrecked; but no, it wasn't that at all.

'Will somebody please, please find Scorcha! I love him! Waaaaaaaah!'

Oh for Jupiter's sake, Hysteria, stick a biscuit in it, will you! **Kraaarrk!**

9. Dust! Wind! Hooves! Noise!

Clamour and confusion! Everyone began
shouting and jostling each other as they tried
to do ten different things at once. I shall never
understand humans. Just when you need to have
a bit of space and quiet to think things through
you go all wipsy-wopsy, waving your arms about
and shouting like a bunch of baboons
in a banana battle.

Primus and Jellus were darting
round each other, throwing punches.

Krysis was standing with his hands on his hips and his chin sticking out, bellowing commands which nobody was interested in. Only Perilus knew what he was doing. He took one look at the chaos all around, quietly picked up a decent-sized helmet and made his way down to the stables, where the horses and chariots were being prepared. I flapped after him, thinking I'd better keep an eye on the young chap.

'Are you sure you can do this, Perilus?'

'No, Croakbag, I'm not sure at all but I've got to try, for Scorcha's sake. Look, why don't you stop following me around and do something useful? Find Scorcha. He can't be all that far away. Find him.'

Kraaarrk! *Toc-toc-toc.* 'Actually, my young friend, that's a good idea. It's not often that you think of somethin' sensible but you have, so well done. I didn't know you had it —'

'Stop babbling and go and find Scorcha!' Perilus yelled, climbing into his chariot. 'I'll do my job, you do yours!'

Of course, the young daredevil was right. I took to the skies. That's the glory of flying, you see, getting the bird's-eye view. I had most of Rome spread below, like jam on a giant slice of bread. I flapped, I swooped, I dived, climbed, glided and flapped some more, keeping my beady eyes on the busy scenes below. There were kids playing by the river, peasants going to the market at the forum, a bunch of people arguing on a doorstep, a house on fire, someone just about to go to the – oops! Don't want to see that, thank you very much! And then, what did I spot but two large figures pulling a strange-looking wardrobe along a track that led to the river.

That's an odd-looking wardrobe, I thought. *I'd better take a look*. The closer I got the more interested I became. The first thing I noticed was that the wardrobe had a large sand timer stuck on the top. It was Maddasbananus's Time Machine! (You remember that one? Another of his inventions that didn't work.)

Then one of the burly figures threw back his hood and – GASP! SURPRISE! – it was none other than Crabbus. I had found The Ghastlies! But what were they doing with Maddasbananus's Time Machine? And why were they planning to dump it in the river?

Was I a bit suspicious? No, I wasn't. I was HIGHLY SUSPICIOUS AND CONCERNED because what was going through my noddle at that moment were two words: WHAT IF? WHAT IF? WHAT IF?

I looked around but there was no help to hand, nobody I could call on for assistance. I was going to have to do this myself and, funnily enough, I was going to enjoy it. There was no time to lose. The Ghastlies were right beside the river and about to topple the wardrobe into the deep and murky waters of the Tiber.

I gained a bit of height first and then I began swooping, diving down on those two Ghastlies, stabbing at them with my whopper of a beak.

'Gerroff!' yelled Crabbus, dropping his side of the wardrobe as he tried to protect himself.

'AARGH!' screeched Septicaemia. 'You dropped the wardrobe on my foot, you fool!'

Then I was attacking her and she managed to drop her side of the wardrobe on her other foot. 'Aaargh! My toes! My little piggy-wigs!'

Not only that, but as the wardrobe hit
the ground again it gave off a muffled yelp.
'MMMMPH!'

There was someone inside! No guessing who
it was. I pecked and pecked at Septicaemia and
Crabbus even faster until at last they gave up
and fled. That left me with the task of untying
the rope that had been wrapped round the Time
Machine. A few
blows with my
rather wonderful
conk and I'd
done it. The
door burst open
and out jumped
Scorcha. There
was a gag over
his mouth and
his hands were
tied. He stood
there, blinking

at the sunlight and staggering about a bit, still rather groggy from whatever it was that had happened to him.

'I don't know what it was,' he said, as I pulled off the gag. 'The Ghastlies put some revolting, smelly rag over my mouth. I got one whiff of it and was almost knocked out.'

'They'd probably soaked it in Stinky Fish Sauce,' I muttered, as I worked at the ropes round his wrists. 'Come on. We have to get you back to the Circus Maximus. Perilus has taken your place in the second heat.'

'Perilus!' cried Scorcha. 'But he's up against champions!'

I shrugged. (Did you know ravens can do that sort of thing? Oh yes, we can shrug all right – *Corvus whoppus shruggia*.) I told Scorcha about Jellus too. 'And I wouldn't be surprised if it was Jellus who put The Ghastlies up for kidnappin' you. You do realize they were goin' to throw you into the river?'

'What!'

'Oh yes. I suppose the Time Machine might have floated for a while, but eventually it would have filled with water and sunk, takin' you with it.'

'That's . . . horrible,' murmured Scorcha. 'I might have –'

'Yes, you might have, but you didn't. Instead we'll get you back to the races and you can get in your chariot, although it's very dangerous and you might – you know?'

Scorcha looked thoughtful. 'It's a funny thing, life, isn't it?'

I nodded. 'That is my general view of things, yes. Come on!'

Well, we got there. Perilus's race was over and we'd missed it all except for the wild cheering as he was declared the winner. Yes, my boy had won! Of course the crowd was chanting 'Scorcha! Scorcha!' thinking it was him. Even Krysis was cheering.

'I've never seen such riding!' he told us as we joined up with the Green Team. 'Perilus was brilliant. Came back from behind, overtook one, two, three chariots! Never seen anything like it! That's my boy!'

'And mine,' I said quietly. 'Maybe you can now see why he wants to be a charioteer.'

Krysis's face darkened. Obviously this wasn't something he was quite ready for yet. I went quiet and let him think on it. It's never a good idea to push something when the door is only slightly open – if you get my meaning.

Scorcha clasped Perilus to his chest and hugged him wildly. They were both grinning like mad. 'You did it! You did it again!' Scorcha told him. 'By Jupiter, Perilus, you're like my guardian angel, stepping in when I most need you. I wish we could get you on the team.'

'That would be my dream come true,' said Perilus, looking across at his father.

I don't think Krysis heard, which was probably

a good thing just at that moment. But I did notice Flavia smiling broadly, her eyes wide with excitement and pleasure at Perilus's victory, and I thought: *Hmmm, maybe Flavia will put in a good word for Perilus with his father*.

Perilus was quickly and unceremoniously pushed out of Scorcha's arms by Hysteria, who now threw herself at the object of her love.

'I was so worried. I thought you'd been killed. (Sniff!) I thought you were dead. (Sniff!) I thought you'd been scrunched by horses, or blown up by a . . . a . . . an asteroid, or eaten by an escaped lion from the Colosseum or there'd been an earthquake and the Pantheon had fallen on you,' she told him, with another big sniff.

'Hysteria! Please! I'm alive, so it's all right now. Please put me down. Let me go now – I've got a race to ride in.'

It was Krysis who pulled his daughter off Scorcha. 'Do you hear? He's got a race to take part in and you, young lady, are meeting Fibbus

Biggus tonight, remember? The man who wants to marry you?'

Hysteria immediately burst into tears. Oh dear. Monsoon season again. However, it did serve to remind me that there was still unfinished business to sort out. It was almost time for me to reveal who the thief was, the thief who had almost destroyed the lives of the dear family that I belonged to – or rather the family that belonged to me, because, let's face it, I was the one sorting everything out, wasn't I? It was me, Croakbag!

The heats soon finished and it was time for the final race, when the five winners would compete for the wreath of laurel leaves and be crowned Chariot Champion of the Roman Empire!

The five chariots were brought to the starting line. Huge cheers went up as the crowds greeted the riders and yelled for their favourites. Every single one of those riders was already a champion in their part of the empire. This was it. This was what Scorcha was up against and he looked so

strong and handsome and brave, standing there
in his chariot. His two beautiful white steeds
stamped nervously at the ground as if they knew
that this was going to be the most important race
of their lives too.

Emperor Tyrannus took hold of the white
starting banner. The shouting and cheering
quickly died away and a deathly hush settled on

the crowd. They craned forward in their seats
so they could see every moment of what was to
come. Some of the horses whinnied quietly. One
blew a snort into the air and pawed the dust.
Their tails whisked at flies. The Emperor raised
the white banner high.

Silence.

The banner dropped.

10. GOGOGOGOGOGOGOGOGO!!!

Scorcha made a brilliant start, but so did two
of the others, Hamiltonia from Britannia and
Vettelus from Germania. Hamiltonia took the
lead quickly with Scorcha right on his tail. The
chariots slid and skidded round the first marker
with the crowd cheering wildly. By the time the
chariots had gone down the straight to the second
marker, Vettelus had pulled up alongside Scorcha
and the two of them swung round the corner
wheel to wheel, with the crowd gasping at such
close riding. It was a miracle that the two chariots
didn't come together and smash each other to
smithereens, in which case it would have been
'SHIPWRECK!'.

It seemed Vettelus had the faster horses
because down the back straight he was pulling

ahead of Scorcha. Scorcha had the inside line on the bend, forcing Vettelus to go wide. The two were concentrating on racing each other so hard that Hamiltonia, with nothing really threatening him, was completely in command of the race.

Scorcha was still losing ground to both Hamiltonia and Vettelus. Half the crowd had gone deathly quiet. Their hero was in third place and falling back. Perilus, watching from the balcony, felt a heavy weight grow in the pit of his stomach. Where was Scorcha? Why wasn't he further ahead? There were only three laps to go.

As Scorcha went thundering past, Perilus
saw him adjust his hold on the reins and take a
different stance on his tiny chariot, planting his
feet firmly right above the spinning axle. There
was a tiny flick on the reins and Scorcha's chariot
suddenly shot forward. His two white steeds
dug in their flashing hooves, pulled their heads
low and stretched out their necks as if willing
themselves to the winning post.

Now it was Scorcha who had to take the
outside line as he caught up with Vettelus.
Neither of them could see that round the next
bend the two chariots that had been running
last had collided with each other, broken apart
and were scattered across half the track. Their
riders were desperately cutting themselves free
from the reins tied round their waists and rushing
towards the edges of the track to avoid being
run over. Hamiltonia had already managed to
squeeze through the wreckage, but it had spread
everywhere – broken wheels, smashed shafts,

splintered axles, crumpled
chariot baskets. And there
were four horses on the
loose too.

Round the bend came Scorcha and Vettelus, neck and neck at full speed. There was only room for one to get past in absolute safety. They were wheel to wheel. There was grinding and sparks flying as they briefly touched and quickly moved apart, but still so close, too close.

And then Scorcha was taking a path through the shattered remains, bumping over some of the smaller pieces, while Vettelus was forced either to slow down and pick his way through or simply go for it at full speed.

That's what Vettelus did because that's what makes a champion. At first it seemed to work and he was three-quarters of the way across, but then one wheel hit a broken axle from one of the shipwrecked chariots and his own chariot lurched and swung from side to side, wilder and wilder, until Vettelus was hurled right out. He hit the ground with a terrible thud and lay still while his horses carried on, pulling his disintegrating chariot as they went careering after Scorcha, who was now flying at full speed after Hamiltonia.

The final lap, and Scorcha was catching up with Hamiltonia but there seemed so little time left to reach him, let alone overtake. Scorcha was flying! Hamiltonia's horses were flagging, their nostrils frothing. The crowd saw him glance behind, keeping a wary eye on Scorcha as the young racer sped towards him.

The last corner and Scorcha was right on the Briton's tail. The crowd erupted. Everyone was on their feet screaming, some for Hamiltonia and even more for their local hero, Scorcha. They were neck and neck, flicking the reins like fury, willing their horses on. The winning line was coming up fast. Scorcha suddenly disappeared from view. No! There he was, crouching down, lying down in his chariot, not even steering, just holding the reins and letting his horses go for it!

The crowd gasped. What was he doing! No charioteer had ever done anything like that. It was madness. You don't win chariot races by lying down! But it was a miracle. The chariot was going even faster. The white horses pulled ahead by a neck and then by a chariot length, then they swooped across the line. Scorcha had won! There he was, standing upright, waving furiously at the hysterical crowd.

Scorcha, Chariot Champion of the Roman Empire!

The horses took him on a lap of honour, and then another lap, and another. The crowd just would not stop cheering. At last, Scorcha pulled his horses to a halt beneath the Emperor's stand. He leaped on to the ground and the first thing he did was go to his horses, thanking each of them before handing them over to one of the stable slaves, who led them away. Then Scorcha mounted the steps to meet the Emperor.

'Rome is proud of you!' declared Tyrannus. 'You have won yourself fame and great riches!' Tyrannus leaned forward and spoke more quietly. 'But not so many riches as me! I had a good bet of money on you, so thank you very much. You had me worried for a while, Scorcha. What on earth were you doing lying down in your chariot? You couldn't even see where you were going!'

'I couldn't think of anything else I could do to make the chariot go faster. The wind was smashing against me and I suddenly thought: *What if I lie down so the wind isn't buffeting me so much? Surely the wind is slowing me.* So I lay down to get out of the wind and it worked! But it was awful down there. There was nothing to cling on to and I was being flung about like a boat among rocks in a storm! I have bruises everywhere.'

Tyrannus smiled and addressed the crowd. 'Well done, champion! And now the wreath. I crown you Scorcha, Chariot Champion of the Roman Empire!'

So that was that, and I was mightily thankful it was all over because my heart had been beating fit to burst right out of my body, and that would not have been a pretty sight at all.

Scorcha went off to the Green Team to celebrate and we headed home. On the way I told my family all about Crabbus and Septicaemia.

'Why would they want to kidnap Scorcha?' demanded Hysteria, who obviously couldn't imagine anyone wanting to harm her beloved in any way at all.

'So he couldn't race,' Krysis explained. 'It's the sort of dirty business that goes on when people start betting on things.'

'That's not fair,' said Hysteria.

'Life isn't fair,' snapped Krysis, which I suppose was fair comment coming from someone who had been falsely accused of robbing the Imperial Mint, flung into jail and thrown out of his lovely villa (four bedrooms, atrium, pool, garden, *et cetera*, *et cetera*), AND had all his money taken away from him. (Did you spot the Latin? Of course you did, brainbox!)

'Don't talk to me about life and fairness,' shouted Hysteria. 'You want to marry me off to some trillion-year-old, bald-headed Fibbus Biggus just because he's got money and we haven't. That's not a very fair way to treat your daughter, especially when you know she loves someone else, is it? Why can't I marry Scorcha? Now that he's Chariot Champion of the Roman Empire he's even richer than Fibbus Biggus!'

'Good point, Hysteria,' I clacked. 'Good for you. Very interestin'. She's quite right there.'

Krysis looked at me as if he wanted to wring my neck. He probably did but I must say I was rather enjoying his discomfort. First of all his son proves to be a mighty fine charioteer and now his daughter wants to marry one!

'Surely I do not have to remind you, Hysteria, that Scorcha is a slave.'

'*Ex*-slave,' Hysteria shot back at her father.

'Now a very rich ex-slave.'

Krysis stopped dead in the road, stuck out his chin and glared at her so hard I thought she might burst into flames. 'Tonight you will have dinner with Fibbus Biggus, Hysteria, and that is the end of this discussion!'

Hysteria's eyes welled up with tears, but she didn't say anything. She simply hung her head in despair and trailed slowly home, her tragic tears splashing silently on to the dusty footprints left by her stern father marching ahead of her. Ah! I really, really should have been a poet. *Corvus poeticus brilliantissimussimussimuss.*

Poor girl. I like Krysis, but sometimes he's a stubborn idiot. There was nothing I could do, at least not yet. There were still plans to be made and people to see and work to be done. It was very hard to keep my beak shut tight, but I couldn't tell anyone, not quite yet. The time for that would come soon. Very soon. Go on, give us a biscuit! **Krraaaarrkkk!**

11. Be Patient!

It must have felt rather strange for poor Flavia
as she bustled round what passed for a kitchen in
the squalid surroundings of their tiny apartment.
After all, she was now preparing a grand supper
for the very man who had taken over the lovely
villa across the road which had been her home
for so many years. And I also wondered how
she felt about the idea of her young daughter
marrying such an ancient, bald bonehead. OK,
so Fibbus Biggus had money, but that was all.

Human beings are very strange sometimes,
and some are stranger than others. And even
as I had that thought, two very strange humans
indeed came bursting into the yard. They were
Crabbus and Septicaemia and as soon as they set
eyes on me they threw themselves towards me.

'You!' screeched Septicaemia. 'Murderer! Villain! Wait until I get my hands round your stinking neck!'

I flapped lightly out of her reach and gazed down at her with my very best innocent stare.

'Me? What are you talking about? What have I done?'

'You tried to kill us! Peck out our eyes! Pull our ears off!' shouted Crabbus.

I shook my feathery head. 'No, no, no, you must be mistaken. It must have been some other raven. We all look much the same, you know. I, of course, have a bigger brain than any other raven, or human for that matter, but apart from that we all look much the same.'

'It was you!' screamed Septicaemia. 'I'd know you anywhere.'

'And I would know you anywhere,' a quiet voice spoke from the gate. It was Scorcha, returning from the celebrations at the Circus Maximus. Scorcha entered the yard and went straight up to The Ghastlies.

'You kidnapped me,' said Scorcha. 'I recognized you even with your hoods up. Apart from anything else it was the smell. You both smell like boiled cabbage. You tried to kidnap me to get me out of the race. So were you betting on Hamiltonia winning? Or, more likely, had someone put you up to it? I think someone didn't want me to win and they sent you to nobble me.'

Septicaemia threw a worried glance at Crabbus and they both shrank back. Scorcha nodded. 'So that was it. No doubt it was Jellus. Yes, yes, I can see from your reaction that I've hit the nail on the head. So Jellus put you up to it. Jellus paid you to nobble me, and you were going to let me drown in the Tiber. I think most people would consider that a pretty big crime. That's why I mentioned it to the Emperor. I have to tell you that Tyrannus is not a happy chappy.'

The Ghastlies threw themselves at Scorcha's feet. 'Take pity on us! Don't let the Emperor throw us to the lions. Please, please, not the lions!' By this time they were both grovelling and sobbing, clutching at Scorcha's sandals. It wasn't a pretty sight.

Scorcha folded his arms across his chest. 'You two don't deserve any mercy. You behave horribly to everyone, you stink, you treat Putuponn like a slave –'

Crabbus lifted his head momentarily. 'But she *is* our slave,' he whimpered.

'Shut up!' hissed Scorcha. 'She is no longer your slave because I shall buy her freedom.'

'You can't do that,' muttered Septicaemia. 'Who will wash the sheets?'

'You can wash the sheets yourself,' Scorcha declared. 'And if I hear any – ANY – complaints about your behaviour from now on I shall go straight back to Tyrannus and he will order your arrest. Now get out of my sight and don't you dare bother any of us ever again. Go on, leave, leave Rome!'

'Yes, yes, master,' muttered Crabbus. He pulled Septicaemia to her feet and they hurried across the yard and out of the gate, then disappeared into the crowds on the street.

I clapped my wings. 'Well done, Scorcha. Justice and mercy together. You'd make a good Emperor!'

Scorcha laughed. 'You're a rascal, Croakbag. You might like to be an Emperor, but I am perfectly happy to be Chariot Champion of the Roman Empire. And now I am going to go and see Krysis and ask if he will allow me to marry Hysteria.'

I shuddered. 'No, no, no, not yet, Scorcha. It's

too soon. Be patient, please. Just wait a few more hours.'

'But Fibbus Biggus is coming this evening to ask for Hysteria's hand. I must ask before him. I don't want to lose Hysteria. I love her.'

'Yes, I know, but you are not in a chariot race now. Things are a lot more complicated. You will have to trust me, Scorcha. Wait until later tonight.'

Scorcha gave me a searching look and then at last gave a little nod. He went off to join Trendia, who was using her kitchen to help Flavia prepare for the big dinner. Wonderful smells were beginning to drift out from both Flavia's and Trendia's kitchens.

There was a curious kind of calm about everything. Hysteria was quiet. Perilus was . . . ? I had no idea where Perilus was. Krysis was preparing the paperwork for Hysteria's marriage agreement with Fibbus Biggus – an agreement that I hoped would never take place.

I decided it was time to pay one more visit to my old friend, the Emperor. Just for once I didn't find Tyrannus in his bath. He was at his desk, counting out all the money he had won by placing a bet on Scorcha to win the chariot champions' race.

Tyrannus welcomed me with open arms. My goodness!

'Croakbag! You were quite right. Scorcha is a real champion. That young man will go far. So, have you brought news about the thief?'

'I know who it is and, just as we thought, it was not Krysis.'

'Then who?'

'All will be revealed very soon, Tyrannus.'

The Emperor shook his head and grunted. 'You do like your little games, don't you, Croakbag? So, if you're not going to tell me, why have you come to see me?'

'Because there is somethin' I need you to do,' I told him bluntly.

'Ah! Of course. Isn't it always the same? You always want me to do something for you, you bag of feathers. So what is it this time?'

'I know an inventor, Maddasbananus. You should see him. Ask him about his fire engine.'

'Fire engine?'

'It's good. It works.'

'Send him to me.'

'Thank you, Tyrannus. And lastly I need you to do this –'

I told him.

'Is that it? That's all? And I shall have the thief?'

'You shall have the thief.'

'Very well. Now be a good bird and flap off while I count my winnings.'

I left him to it – the king in his counting house, counting out his money. Humans, eh? I was suddenly glad that I had no interest in money at all. Dead squirrels and squashed rats, yes, but money? No.

It was already evening when I got back to the grotty apartment that passed for a home. I could hear an argument taking place. Perilus was quarrelling with his father. Scorcha was there too.

'But I don't want to be a lawyer,' Perilus shouted. 'I want to be a charioteer.'

'No.' Krysis really did stamp his foot.

'The thing is,' said Scorcha, 'the Green Team want Perilus to join them.'

'No,' Krysis repeated.

'The Green Team don't make any offer like that lightly,' Scorcha pointed out. 'It's a great honour to be asked. And Perilus will be paid too.'

'No.'

Scorcha didn't give up. 'You saw for yourself how well Perilus raced. He won that heat. If it hadn't been for Perilus I would never have become champion. Perilus is a natural charioteer. He was born to race on wheels. Please, Krysis, at least think about it. Don't dismiss it out of hand. Consider what it means. Perilus – as a good charioteer – could end up being far richer than any lawyer. So please, at least give it some consideration.'

Krysis looked at Perilus and then Scorcha and then Perilus again. He took a deep breath. 'I will think about it,' he said at last and swept from the room.

Scorcha smiled, but Perilus looked pretty miserable. I landed on his shoulder.

'Cheer up, Perilus. I have a feelin' that your father may well change his mind.'

'Pater never changes his mind,' Perilus grunted.

'Have I ever let you down?' I asked.

'Yes,' Perilus snapped back. 'Several times.'

'Oh. Well, forget about those. So, apart from them, have I ever let you down?'

Perilus shook his head. 'There we are then. Everythin' will be all right. Just be patient.'

Whaddya mean, you're fed up because I keep telling everyone to be patient but nothing happens? Like I said, be patient! And stop interrupting too, so I can get on with things. Get over it! **Kraaaarrkk!**

12. Marriage? What Marriage? Whose Marriage?

Toc-toc-toc! Flavia had gone mad with the food. I'd never seen so many pizzas – cheese pizzas, tomato pizzas, cheese and tomato pizzas, cheese and cheese pizzas, cheese and tomato and cheese pizzas, *ad infinitum*. Yes, it's the old Latin again. Aren't you going to be a clever clogs? *Ad infinitum*. It means – more or less – 'again and again', or 'until the end of time'.

Come to think of it, there was a lot of *ad infinitum* about Hysteria's weeping, poor girl. I could hear her up in the room above, crying her heart out as the time for the marriage deal with Fibbus Biggus approached.

Don't think I am unsympathetic. Us ravens might seem black-hearted but, just like you

140

humans, you have to look beneath the feathers and into our hearts. Do I have a black heart? No. (Actually, I have no idea what colour my heart is nor do I wish to know because I would much rather keep it safe and sound in my chest, where it can beat away happily keeping me alive, thank you very much.)

Anyhow, if anyone was going to save Hysteria from being sentenced to life imprisonment in a marriage with Fibbus Biggus, it was going to be me. Oh yes. I am not called *Corvus maximus intelligentissimus* for nothing. Did anyone else have a plan? No, they didn't. Did I have a plan? Oh yes. And it was a very good plan that would make me a hero. I might even be given my own crown of laurel leaves or, even better, a treasure chest full of dead squirrels and some yummy, chewy dead rats and mice. **Kraaaarrrkkk!**

Meanwhile Flippus Floppus and Fussia were still bustling backwards and forwards with pizzas and other titbits for the table until there was no space left on it. Krysis came to inspect everything. He'd put on his smartest white and yellow toga and he looked quite the best biscuit. (That's what one of my aunts used to say about anything special. She'd clack her beak, *toc-toc-toc*, and say, 'Well, she thinks she's quite the best biscuit, doesn't she?')

Krysis gave me a dark look. 'If you so much as nibble ANYTHING on that table I'll wring your neck, Croakbag.'

'That's a very nice greetin', Krysis. Good evenin' to you too.' I honoured him with a polite nod.

'I know you,' Krysis went on. 'I hope you haven't got anything up your sleeve that will annoy me on this very important occasion.'

I spread my wings wide. 'My dear Krysis, as you can see, I don't have any sleeves at all.'

Kraaarrkkk! Good raven joke, eh?

Whaddya mean, a worm could make better jokes than that? Can worms speak? Can they

142

even think? I doubt it very much. Mind you, Krysis didn't think it was funny either.

'Where's Perilus? Have you put him up to some trick or other?'

I know I can be a bit crafty at times but this was way beyond me. I had no idea where Perilus was. In fact, I hadn't seen him since that argument with his father.

'Nothin' to do with me,' I told Krysis, with a shrug. 'Have you lost him?'

'The boy's been out for hours,' Krysis complained. 'He's supposed to be here. His sister's marriage contract is a major family ceremony.'

There was a strange noise from Hysteria's room. It was the sound of silence. She had stopped crying. That was quite odd, but things suddenly got even odder as the whole apartment began to shudder.

'Earthquake!' Krysis shouted as Flavia hurried into the room and they clutched at each other

for safety. Flippus Floppus and Fussia both threw
themselves under the table.

I, of course, knew it couldn't possibly be an
earthquake. Us animals are very much in tune
with Nature and can easily tell the difference
between an earthquake and something even more
unexpected. Something was battering against
the wooden house, and because the building
was so old and rickety it was making the whole
place shake. So, while Krysis and Flavia panicked
inside, I zipped outside to see what was going on.

I almost broke my beak flying into something
large, grey and very tough. It was an elephant,

parked right outside the house and bumping gently against the outer wall. No wonder the building was shuddering to bits! Sitting on top of the elephant was Perilus. He was right in the middle of trying to persuade Hysteria to jump out of her window on to Tiddles's back.

'Then you can elope with Scorcha!' he whispered loudly. 'Come on, jump!'

Hysteria was perched on her window ledge, looking scared but determined and ready to throw herself on to the pachyderm.

Oh dear! This was all I needed. This would scupper my plans good and proper. What's more, it would cause more of a problem than it would solve. The last thing I wanted to see was an elephant scampering about the countryside with Hysteria and Perilus on its back.

'Perilus! Perilus! Stop this at once! It's not a good idea.'

'It's a very good idea, Croakbag,' Perilus shot back. 'I'm going to rescue Hysteria and she can run away with Scorcha on Tiddles and they'll be happy for ever and ever.'

'But I've already got a much better plan in place. For the sake of Jupiter and all the other gods will you please take Tiddles away?'

'No way! I'm going to rescue my sister! Come on, Hysteria, JUMP!'

I would have to do something. I didn't want to do it but I could see twelve chapters of hard work going wrong if I didn't. I whizzed upwards, turned on my tail and came diving back down like a rocket. This was going to hurt – me! I aimed straight for Tiddles's backside – and let's face it, her rear end was a pretty big target so I couldn't miss. I just hoped that Perilus was holding on tight.

Full speed, the wind whistling through my feathers . . . and I stabbed into Tiddles's bottom with my sharp beak. OOOOFFF! It felt as if my beak had been pushed into the back of my head but it did the job. Tiddles was so surprised and

stung by my attack that she took off at high speed with Perilus clinging to one very large ear. Off went the elephant, charging out of the yard and up the road.

At much the same time Krysis and Flavia came rushing out of the house to see what was going on.

'What was that?' cried Krysis, peering up the now empty road.

'Wha-wha-wha?' I asked, barely able to speak because my beak felt so bent, broken and generally out of order.

'What's the matter with you?' Krysis demanded. 'Can't speak? Oh good.' He turned to Flavia. 'Earthquake seems to have finished. Obviously just a small one. We'd better get back inside. Fibbus Biggus will be with us at any moment.'

It's a good thing they went back in before they spotted Hysteria still perching on her window ledge. I flew up to her and pointed with one wing. 'Inside! Now! Just do whatever your father says and I promise you everythin' will be all right. Now I must go.'

Phew. Problems, problems! If only everyone listened to me instead of each other the world would be a much safer place and there'd be no nonsense to deal with. By Jupiter, this family of

148

mine seemed to cause more problems than an entire enemy army. I had no idea where Perilus and Tiddles had got to but I was pretty sure they would be OK.

But now I could see Fibbus Biggus crossing the road and he was about to arrive and collect his bride. He raised a chubby fist and knocked loudly on the front door, which immediately fell off. (I told you the entire apartment was rotting away.) Fibbus Biggus stepped across the fallen door, holding his nose against the clouds of dust that rose up from the floor.

'Fibbus, welcome,' greeted Krysis, bowing low. How he must have hated doing that. Krysis was, after all, Fibbus's old boss until someone, SOMEONE I KNEW, stole 10,000 silver denarii from the Imperial Mint and Krysis had taken the rap.

'Krysis,' murmured Fibbus Biggus, turning his head to one side in an attempt to avoid looking at him. 'Is the girl here?'

How rude! *'Is the girl here?'* Fibbus Biggus couldn't even say Hysteria's name. He was treating her as if she was a pot or a pan that he wanted to buy. And of course he was '*buying*' her. I could see his servant carrying a large money bag.

'I shall fetch her,' murmured Flavia, and she went to Hysteria's room. A few moments later they both came out. Hysteria hung her head and stared at the floor.

My heart was beginning to race. I thought everyone in the room would be able to hear it but they were too busy watching Hysteria and Fibbus.

Flavia smiled at Fibbus. 'Fibbus, please, sit down and eat.'

'Fetch the documents first,' Fibbus demanded. 'We'll eat afterwards.'

Krysis pulled out the rolled papyrus. It was bound with a dark blue ribbon, which Krysis now untied. He unrolled the parchment and Fibbus read through it.

'It seems to be correct. Is the girl ready to sign?'

'Her name is Hysteria,' I croaked up loudly and Krysis shot me a warning look.

Fibbus stared at me. 'Is that creature yours?'

'Apparently, but not for much longer if he keeps misbehaving,' muttered Krysis.

'I hate birds,' said Fibbus.

'I'm not all that fond of some humans,' I told him.

Fibbus ignored me. 'Fetch the pen,' he snapped and Krysis duly leaned across and offered him a quill. Fibbus snatched at it and scribbled his signature at the end of the document.

A faint noise of footsteps in the yard alerted me. Good. Somebody outside. Just in time.

'Now the girl signs,' Fibbus ordered and Hysteria approached the desk. She took the quill from Fibbus and glanced angrily at her father. This was the moment I'd been waiting for, at last!

Krraaarrkkk!

12½. All Done and Dusted.
Go on, Give Us a Biscuit!

Er-hrrrm-fffmph. That was me clearing my throat
to get attention. It worked. Everyone turned and
stared at me as I flapped down to the little desk
and fixed Fibbus Biggus with one beady eye. (I
can only do one beady eye at a time, on account
of my eyes being on the sides of my head, rather
than at the front.) I fluffed up my feathers and
took up my most important stance, *id est* one foot
slightly in front of the other and head cocked
enquiringly to one side. (*Id est* – 'that is to say'.
And that is to say it is my last bit of Latin for you.)

'Just one moment,' I began. 'There is a bit of a
problem.'

'What's that stupid bird of yours on about?'
asked Fibbus Biggus.

'I will tell you what I'm on about. I believe the law says that criminals can't marry.' I kept my very beady eye on Fibbus.

'What criminal? Surely the girl –'

'Hysteria,' I corrected.

'– isn't a criminal?'

'Of course she isn't,' Krysis declared.

'Of course she isn't,' I repeated. 'You are the criminal, Fibbus. It was you who stole the money from the Imperial Mint.'

'Me! Don't be ridiculous! The money was found in Krysis's bedroom, hidden away beneath his bed. He was practically caught in the act. How could it possibly be me? It's Krysis who is the criminal!'

Krysis stared at me, his eyes bulging, not knowing what to think or who to believe.

'Croakbag?' he croaked, sounding more like me than me. 'What's going on?'

'It's quite simple really. Fibbus Biggus stole the money and when the soldiers came to search the villa it was one of the soldiers who hid the money and then immediately "found" it. He was Fibbus's accomplice.'

Fibbus had turned very red and was spluttering all over the place. 'It's a preposterous lie! I had nothing to do with it. It wasn't me. It was the soldier!'

'I'm not so sure,' I went on, quite calmly. I was in charge of the situation, you see, me, Croakbag, a mere raven, but *Corvus superbia detectivus*. 'Let's ask the soldier.'

I went to the broken door and invited three newcomers to enter the house. In they came, the Imperial Guard, our old friends Plausible, Ludicrus and Ridiculus.

Fibbus immediately pointed a finger at Ludicrus. 'He did it! That one!'

Ludicrus pulled off his helmet. 'He told me to. Fibbus Biggus stole the money and said he'd pay me a thousand denarii to hide it in the man's bedroom and then pretend to find it stashed away

there. But Fibbus hasn't paid me anything yet, not a single coin. He's a cheat and a liar and a thief.'

Krysis drew himself up to his full height. 'Guards, arrest that guard – and also arrest this man here,' he ordered, pointing an accusing finger at Fibbus Biggus.

Plausible and Ridiculus did their work and

marched the two criminals away into the dark of the evening.

Krysis turned to me. 'How did you know?' he asked me.

'We always knew it wasn't you,' I explained. 'It was just a matter of findin' out who really did it. One of the prisoners from the jail overheard Ludicrus talkin' about what he'd done. After that it was simply a matter of puttin' two and two together.'

Krysis looked at me in silence for a long time. I could see it was hard for him to say what he said next. 'Thank you, Croakbag.'

Hysteria put down the quill she was still holding. 'Does this mean I don't have to marry Fibbus Biggus?'

'There is no way I would allow any daughter of mine to marry such a man,' Krysis told her.

'Except that ten minutes ago you were about to do just that,' Hysteria pointed out. 'Yes, well, since you obviously aren't fit to choose a husband for me perhaps you will let me do it myself, in which case I choose Scorcha. Thank you very much.'

'But, but, but,' began Krysis.

'No "buts" now,' Flavia put in. 'Can't you see they love each other? Let them be.'

At that point Perilus came bursting into the house, panting furiously, so he'd definitely been running.

'DON'T SIGN THE MARRIAGE DOCUMENT!' he yelled at Hysteria.

'Silly boy! I haven't,' Hysteria calmly answered.

I did think that was a bit much, her calling Perilus a silly boy. I mean to say, he was the one who had tried to save her with Tiddles the elephant. OK, so it wasn't a very good plan but at least Perilus had tried.

Perilus could tell from our faces that something big had happened – well, perhaps he couldn't tell from my face, but he could read his family's faces, and Fussia's and Flippus Floppus's.

'What happened?' Perilus demanded.

'Fibbus Biggus was unmasked as the thief,' grinned Krysis.

'By me,' I put in.

'And Ludicrus has been arrested too because he was unmasked as Fibbus's accomplice,' added Krysis.

'By me,' I put in again.

'All right!' snapped Krysis. 'Croakbag . . . helped.'

'Helped?' I squeaked. 'HELPED? Is that all you think I did? I HELPED?'

Flavia slipped one arm round Krysis's waist. She smiled at me. 'I think Croakbag has been magnificent. Don't you agree, darling? After all, he is quite right. He found out about Ludicrus and it was Croakbag who knew that Fibbus Biggus was the thief.'

Krysis glared at me and heaved a long sigh. 'Oh, I suppose so. Here, have a biscuit,' he muttered as he threw one across to me.

'I am deeply honoured,' I said, mustering up as much dignity as I could under the trying circumstances I was being subjected to.

'Knock knock,' said someone at the door who couldn't actually knock on the door as it was lying in pieces on the floor, as you may well remember.

A guard marched in. It was Namelus. Was this going to be more trouble?

'I bear a message from Emperor Tyrannus to Krysis, Master of the Imperial Mint,' stated the guard and he handed across a rolled parchment.

Krysis undid the seal and read it. A smile spread across his face. 'I have been given my job back as Master of the Mint, and my villa and fortune have all been restored.'

'Because of me,' I couldn't help adding and everyone turned and yelled:

'CROAKBAG! SHUT UP! YOU GREAT BLACK BLABBER-BEAK!'

'I was only sayin',' I muttered.

Well, you can imagine the celebrations we

had. We ate ALL the pizzas Flavia had baked.
We danced round the table. We danced ON
the table, until it broke of course, as you would
expect, and we all fell to the ground and rolled
about laughing. Hysteria was crying, as usual, but
this time they were tears of laughter and joy.

The very next day we moved back to the villa, in style. Krysis had hired a band to come and play as we marched ceremoniously across the road and back into the old villa – OUR villa, our home.

Perilus went and fetched Tiddles and parked her in the garden.

'Are you sure she'll be all right?' asked Flavia, as she watched Tiddles live up to her name beside a small tree.

'We could make the garden bigger, couldn't we, Pater?' suggested Perilus.

'Hmmm,' Krysis answered, rather ambiguously.

Scorcha and Maddasbananus and Trendia all came to help us move back in.

Maddasbananus was very happy because he had received news that the Emperor wanted to see how his fire engine worked. And while Scorcha was moving some of our furniture from one room to another he mentioned once more that the Green Team would very much like to speak to Krysis and his son, Perilus, about the boy joining their team – if they were interested.

'And I am very interested!' shouted Perilus, who was jumping up and down with excitement at the news.

Flavia could see that Krysis was finding it very hard to make this decision, so she stepped in to help. 'Why not let Perilus have a go? If he fails then there will still be plenty of time for him to take up his studies as a lawyer, like you. But look at him, Krysis: he's only eleven. He wants to be a charioteer. It's what he's always wanted and we know he's good.'

'He's not good,' Scorcha butted in. 'He's VERY GOOD – a future champion.'

'I'd have to beat you to be a champion,' Perilus said with great seriousness.

'That day will come,' Scorcha predicted and smiled.

Krysis crumpled. 'Very well,' he agreed.

So, let's leave things there, eh? Everything was going to be all right. Hysteria was engaged to Scorcha, Perilus would join the Green Team, Fibbus Biggus was in jail with Ludicrus, Maddasbananus was on the verge of becoming a rich inventor, Trendia had found a wonderful new husband, Krysis was back as Master of the Imperial Mint and Tiddles was busy eating the entire villa garden. Perfect!

And nearly all of it was because of me, Croakbag, the most brilliant, intelligent and masterful raven the Roman world had ever known. Go on, chuck us several biscuits!

KRAAARRRRKKKK!!